THE HALLS OF CARSON HIGH
BOOK ONE

I0553007

Riverside Redemption

Rebecca M. Norris

Duskraven Entertainment, LLC

This is a work of fiction. Names, characters, businesses, events and incidents are the products of the author's imagination. Any resemblance to actual persons, living or dead, or actual events is purely coincidental. This novel's story and characters are fictitious. Certain long-standing institutions, agencies, and public offices are mentioned, but the characters involved are wholly imaginary.

Copyright © 2022 Rebecca M. Norris.

To request permissions, contact the author at admin@rebeccanorrisbooks.com.

Hardcover ISBN: 979-8-9850971-3-9
Paperback ISBN: 979-8-9850971-2-2

Library of Congress Control Number: 2021925030

First paperback edition May 2022.

Edited by Scott Norris
Layout by Rebecca M. Norris
Cover designed by GetCovers.com

Scripture quotations taken from The Holy Bible, New International Version® NIV® Copyright © 1973 1978 1984 2011 by Biblica, Inc. TM. Used by permission. All rights reserved worldwide.

Printed by Duskraven Entertainment, LLC in the USA.

Duskraven Entertainment, LLC
PO Box 3795
Olathe, KS 66063

www.rebeccanorrisbooks.com

Acknowledgements

I want to give a very special thank you to all of the people and organizations that are working hard to rescue the lost and traumatized young people in our society and around the world. For the safety of those involved I won't mention names, but they *are* out there and they do amazing things in order to save the children that are sold into trafficking, kidnapped, abused, and have fallen prey to so many other horrible fates.

I have had the very special and humbling experience of aiding one of these organizations personally, and donating to several others. What I have learned has forever changed my life. The people I have met are true heroes who have gone to great lengths, including risking and sacrificing their own lives, in order to bring these lost children home.

To all of you, I say thank you.

This book is dedicated to all of the children and young people suffering at the hands of others. There is still hope, there is help, just hold on...

1

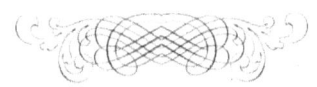

The hallways of Carson High School quickly emptied after another grueling day of algebra problems and scientific lab experiments. The immaculate building with its wide hallways and antiquated architecture looked like a skeleton in a matter of minutes as 1643 students gathered their belongings and started home.

Bruce Weber, a self-proclaimed eternal tough guy, wandered down the locker rows in a lackadaisical manner. There were multiple holes in his jeans, paint stains, and patches. He always wore two or three t-shirts at the same time; short-sleeved over long, usually in orange or blue. His brown hair had been dyed black one too many times. Combat boots and a leather jacket thrown over his shoulder completed the look.

Bruce seldom had a nice word to say to anyone and was known as the town bully. He would knock the books out of people's hands and laugh as the poor souls gathered them together again. Sometimes he would snatch one and hide it just to see what would happen. Bruce had a few followers but was not liked by the general population of Riverside.

On this particular September day Bruce decided he needed someone to annoy. He turned down another row of lockers and spotted Julianne Marie Hathaway.

Julie was the exact opposite of Bruce. She was named "Most Considerate" by her peers. Julie was the type who would pick up the books Bruce has just knocked out of someone's hands, or help them find their books again. She was always well dressed and carried a sweater tied around her waist in case she got a chill later on in the day. She wore her thick, long auburn hair in a ponytail, yet wisps always appeared by midday. She never wore make-up because to her, it was a waste of time and money. She was the envy of all the girls and the object of the boys' affections. Naturally, she would be the latest

2

victim in Bruce's reign of terror.

Oh no! Thought Julie, *Not today! Maybe he will just ignore me.*

"See somethin' interesting, Hathaway?" Bruce asked and gave her a sinister stare.

"No, Bruce." Julie replied, "I just happened to look up as you came around the corner. Don't get so worked up."

He didn't reply, just continued to glare at her.

"See that it doesn't happen again, got it?" He reached into her locker, hooked her books with his hand and pulled them onto the floor. "Oops!"

"Argh! Bruce! There was no reason to do that! I haven't done anything to you!" Julie fumed. She picked up her books and replaced them in her locker.

"It was an accident. Honest." He said as he walked backwards down the hall. He laughed and turned the corner.

She decided to just leave instead of confronting him, and headed for the front doors. She stormed out of Carson High at an alarming pace and went straight to her car, a cute little car with a soft beige color and matching interior. She turned on her favorite station and turned up the volume, drowning herself in the latest songs. *Just 31 more weeks and I'll be rid of him for life!* She thought as she turned down her street. She repeated the words

3

to herself as she walked in the back door and fixed her favorite snack, a potato chip sandwich and a diet soda.

She had just settled down in one of the wingback chairs to watch her favorite show when the phone on the credenza rang.

"Hello?" she asked in her kindest voice.

"Hey, Hathaway." It was Bruce. *Will he ever leave me alone?* "You ran off before I could tell ya somethin'," he continued.

"What did you want, Bruce?" she asked, trying to be friendly and patient.

"BURRRP!"

"Gross! Bruce, grow up!"

"No, wait—"

SLAM! She was thoroughly disgusted and did not hear him try to apologize.

She tried to go back to watching TV, but she couldn't get that phone call out of her mind. Why did the school board insist on distributing everyone's home phone number in the school directory? She flipped aimlessly through the channels completely disinterested in anything she might like to watch.

He wasn't always like this, she thought, *I wonder why he changed? He used to be such a good person. Maybe he just needs a friend. Sure hope he finds one because it isn't*

4

going to be me! She decided to call her best friend, Laurie Whitcomb, to see if she wanted to hang out.

Lauren Paige Whitcomb has lived across the street and two doors down from Julie their whole lives. They used to play dolls together when they were two, and later invited each other over for "tea." They did everything together and it got to the point where they knew each other's thoughts they were that close.

They were also very much alike. Laurie was as well dressed as Julie. She kept her golden curls piled atop her head like a crown and only occasionally wore them down around her shoulders. Julie and Laurie differed in one respect. Laurie simply *couldn't* be seen without her make-up on even though her dark blue eyes with violet flecks were enough to light up her face. Both Julie and Laurie were tall and both were skinnier than beanpoles. Laurie had a 4.1 GPA with weighted college courses, and she was co-captain of the cheerleading squad. She was also a member of the schools golf and diving teams. Where she found the time for all her many activities no one will ever know.

To this trusted friend of a lifetime Julie confided. After all, Laurie disliked Bruce more than she did. She dialed the number and Laurie answered on the fifth ring.

"Hi Laurie. Guess what."

"What?" She sounded a little sleepy. Julie was afraid she had awakened her.

"I hope I didn't wake you, but Bruce Weber just called me and belched into the phone!" Her stomach churned at the thought of the call Bruce had just given her.

"Yuck! What'd he do that for?!" Laurie was fully awake now, and almost as disgusted as Julie had been.

"Do I know? Listen Laur, I need to get out. Let's go to a movie or something."

"Sure... Oh wait! I promised to go to the movies with Dave tonight."

"Oh! Okay! Well, do you think we could double?"

"Yeah, he probably won't mind. Who would you bring?"

"I'll ask Neal. I haven't talked to him in a few days, and you know how much fun the four of us have together."

"Okay. Sounds great! I'll call you back in about fifteen minutes. Bye!"

It was all set. They were going out to see the new murder-mystery, "Deep Submersion," and then grab a bite to eat at Mario's afterward.

Neal was the first to arrive at Julie's house. Neal Sutherland lived in the exquisite house next to Julie's. It was almost entirely made out of brick and stone. It had six bedrooms each with its own bathroom and costly furniture. Fine old antiques of the ages filled the living and dining rooms. It had a six-car garage and was built on the corner so there was plenty of yard space. Oriental rugs and expensive tapestries completed the look that Mrs. Sutherland intended.

It was from this house that he had emerged with a happy gait, whistling his favorite tune. Neal was the laid-back type. He always wore jeans and a t-shirt or sweater depending on the weather. His dark brown hair was cut close and he always had a smile on his face. Neal had lived next door to Julie and across the street and three houses down from Laurie their whole lives. He used to carry their books home from the elementary school for them, and invite them over to play his latest video games. The three of them did a lot together. To Neal, they were his sisters and always would be, but Neal was never as close to Julie as was Laurie.

Neal loved cars and worked on them whenever he had the opportunity. Whether it was a station wagon or a go-cart he was always under the hood. He carried a greasy towel in his back pocket and usually had a wrench in the other. He was also a 4.0 student, but like Bruce, was not liked by the general population of

Riverside, but for different reasons. The Sutherlands were aristocratic and turned their noses at other, less fortunate people. Neal often thought he was adopted he is so unlike his family. Unfortunately, his lot fell with them and he was stuck.

He walked across the lawn to Julie's back door and let himself in. Hardly anyone in Riverside locked their doors.

"Hey, Jules!"

"Hi, Neal. The others aren't here yet, but grab yourself a sandwich if you like."

He liked, and made a monstrous sandwich of cheese, tomato, lettuce, turkey, and corned beef, with a mountain of mayo and mustard. He grabbed a plate and napkin and headed for the all-white, high-quality Hathaway sofa.

"So, what are we going to watch?" he said as he sat down with a thump next to Julie. He thought for a minute and got up again. "Forgot a drink!" he said and gave Julie his most winning smile.

This brought merriment to Julie's deep gray eyes and she laughed. "I was thinking we could go see 'Deep Submersion' and maybe grab a bite to eat."

"That's cool. We going in David's car?"

"Good question. I hadn't thought about that."

"What?! Julie Hathaway stumped? Ha-ha!"

"Hush up! Yes, we'll go in David's car. So there!" She gave him a playful punch in the arm as he finished his sandwich.

Laurie and David drew up about a quarter to five, sauntered up the walk, and let themselves in. David Hawthorne was a freshman this year at the university on the other side of the mountains. He'd been dating Laurie for about two years. They met at the Homecoming Dance Laurie's sophomore year, David's junior. One might call it "love at first sight." Their eyes met across a crowded dance floor and he walked over to meet her, tripped and spilled punch all over his suit! Laurie came to help him up and they've been together ever since. David was a bit of a jock. He was a receiver on the Varsity football team all four years of high school and he played baseball in the spring. He won a football scholarship and barely had time to sleep, let alone do his homework. His life motto has always been "Okay, I'm game!" and he usually was. He hadn't been home at all since he left mid-summer and can only stay the weekend. Julie was flattered that he wanted to go to the movies instead of spending every waking moment with Laurie.

"Hello, Neal! Good to see ya! And how is Miss Hathaway this fine evening?" He bowed low and Julie

9

couldn't resist punching him playfully.

"Knock it off," she said, "and to answer your question, I'm disgusted. You remember Bruce Weber, don't you, David?"

"Yeah, what of him?"

"He has started to pick on me again. He called about an hour ago."

"Say no more. Let's go before he calls again," he opened the door, "Mademoiselle? Monsieur?" He escorted Laurie and Neal out to his new SUV, a graduation present from his parents.

"I'll be there in a minute," said Julie, "I have to tell my mom I'm going out." She dialed the number to her mother's advertising agency and waited for the receptionist to transfer her.

"Hi, Mom! Listen, I'm going out with Neal, David, and Laurie. We're going to a movie. I should probably be home by nine or ten. Is that okay? Thanks, by the way, where's Jo? Oh she's at Katie's house. Is she walking home? All right, see you later. Love ya! Bye!" She headed out to David's car and got in the backseat with Neal. They decided to go to Mario's first and catch the later movie.

Julie had finally forgotten the events of the afternoon by the time they left the theater. She thought she heard her name, but decided she didn't.

"Julie! Hey, Hathaway!"

She did hear her name. She turned around and there was Bruce. He stood next to his bike as if he were waiting for her. He gave her a cocky smile and patted the seat. Julie wanted to scream, but instead she felt an arm around her waist, propelling her towards David's car. Good ol' Neal had rescued her once again.

She waved a superficial greeting and they left. Bruce was left standing next to his motorcycle.

They were silent on the way home waiting for Julie to talk.

"He makes me so mad! It is so *hard* to be kind to him!" she said at last.

"You just give me the word and I'll punch him full of holes, Julie."

"Thanks, David, but I don't think that will help any." She sighed and looked at all the passing homes and shops.

"It probably won't, but I wouldn't mind anyway!" That brought riotous laughter from everyone and Julie thought to herself, *David always knows how to lighten the mood!*

David dropped Neal and Julie off and then went on to Laurie's house.

"Thanks, Neal, for rescuing me."

"Hey, no sweat. That's what I'm here for! G'night, Jules. Sweet dreams."

"Good night," and they parted.

Julie opened the garage door and walked into the living room.

At the sound of the door opening her mother looked up from the magazine she was reading and greeted her.

"Hi, honey, how was the movie?"

"It was pretty good. I think you and Dad should go see it." Julie put her jacket on the hook and walked over to her mother.

"Where is your sister?" Cynthia asked.

"What do you mean? She isn't here?" asked Julie and sat in a chair across from her mother. "You said she was walking home, right?"

"Yes, but she isn't here. I thought you decided to take her with you. Maybe she's still at Katie's."

Just then the phone rang.

"Hello? Oh, hi, Katie. Say is Johannah still there? She left your house hours ago? When? Five o'clock! No, she isn't here. I thought she was with you. Did she say where she was going? No? Okay, thanks Katie. No, that's okay. I'm sure she'll walk in any minute now. Bye!"

"Julie, what was that all about?" asked an alarmed Mrs. Hathaway. She set the magazine down and walked over to her eldest daughter.

"I don't know, Mom. Katie said Jo left her house at five. She should have been here by now; it's just down the street. Maybe she's at Erin's house. Do you want me to call?"

"Please. If she's there tell her to come straight home. Better yet, tell her I'll come pick her up. It's pretty dark."

But Johannah wasn't at Erin's house. Nine o'clock turned to ten o'clock and ten to eleven and still no Johannah.

"She does this all the time!" Julie said, exasperated by her sister's blatant actions. "Why does she do this?" It was a statement more than a question.

"I don't know," Mrs. Hathaway said. "Sometimes I think she does it on purpose. She is so reckless! She just doesn't understand it isn't safe to wander off at her age, at any age!"

"I'll go drive around and see if I can find her." Julie grabbed her keys and started towards the garage door.

"No, you stay here in case she comes home. I'll go look for her." She took her keys off the hook and left.

Julie wondered to herself what her sister could be thinking to stay out so late. Of course she often takes off without word to anyone, but it just wasn't like her to stay out past nine without telling *someone*. She went upstairs and brought down her devotional, then settled into the sofa with the cordless phone and her cell phone beside her. She said a quick prayer that her irresponsible little sister was somewhere safe for the night and would call or come home in the morning.

Julie noticed the message indicator flashing on the cordless phone. *That's strange, there's a message. Why didn't I notice it before! I bet that's Jo!* She dialed the passcode and listened to the message. It was from someone named Mrs. O'Halloran thanking her mother for letting Jo stay the night and promising that she was safe at their house. She could hear her sister laughing in the background. Julie quickly called her mother's cell and told her of the message.

"Oh, thank goodness!" She exclaimed, obvious relief in her voice. "I was just about to call the police! I'm on my way home. Go to bed, sweetheart, thank you."

Julie hung up the phone, waited until she heard her mother's car pull up, and then went upstairs. As she prepared for bed she heard her mother softly pacing below. Eventually Mrs. Hathaway settled down and put on some soft music.

Jo, can't you see what you've done? She thought to her sister. *Mom is worried sick and you know better! Why do you constantly do this? Why do you insist on being so*

14

rebellious?

Sometime later Dr. Hathaway came in after making his rounds at the hospital and asked why Mrs. Hathaway looked so worried.

"I just don't know what to do about Johannah," she said, a crease forming in her brow. "She went off again without telling anyone, George." She stood up and started pacing back and forth across the living room again.

He muttered something unintelligible, and Julie could hear him take a deep breath before sitting down. She could imagine him with his head in his hands, thinking.

That was all Julie heard before she fell into a restless sleep.

2

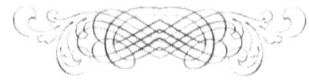

When Julie woke up unusually late the next morning, she found Jo sitting at the breakfast table while her parents yelled. She came in quietly and got herself a bowl of cereal.

"Didn't you read my note, Mom?" Jo asked, and wondered why she was in so much trouble.

"What note? Johannah Selene, there wasn't any note!" Mrs. Hathaway was wringing her hands and tried to steady her voice, but failed. Both Dr. and Mrs. Hathaway were in the same clothes they had on last night. Julie suspected they had been up all night talking about Jo.

"The note I left by the phone. I put it there figuring someone would see it. It said I was going to spend the night at Shauna's house. Didn't you see it?" Jo asked as she walked over to the phone.

"No, I didn't see any note. Julie was the first to use the phone last night. Julie, did you see it?" asked Mrs. Hathaway as she turned towards her eldest daughter.

"No, Mom, there wasn't a note when I used the phone." She said. Julie decided to go search the living room while the discussion continued. She found the note under the sofa and brought it to her father.

Dr. Hathaway read the note, went over to the table, sat down, and handed it to his wife.

"Here Cynthia, read it." He faced his youngest child. "You know, this means nothing at all. You should have called us and gotten our permission. This note does not excuse your behavior in the slightest bit! What were you thinking? We don't even know this person! You could have been hurt, don't you see that?"

Jo finally gave up trying to convince her parents everything was fine and sat down to a cold omelet and warm juice.

After she read the note Cynthia looked puzzled. Finally she asked, "Who is Shauna? How long have you known her? If her mother hadn't called us we would never have known where you were. Do you have any idea how worried we were? Who are these people you so graciously decided not to inform us of?"

"She's new," explained Johannah, "Her family moved down here Monday. They have the house at the end of the block. She's really nice and she has the most beautiful red hair. Get this, Mom, she has emeralds for eyes! You've just got to meet her." To Julie's ear it sounded as if her sister still didn't understand how serious the situation truly was.

The phone rang then and Julie went to answer the extension in the study so she wouldn't be overheard.

It was Laurie on the phone, bright and cheerful as usual.

"Hey Julie! Tried your cell, no answer. Listen, I was thinking about going to the mall later. I need more eye shadow, and besides, I want to check out that new store. Wanna come?"

"Sorry Laurie. Jo did her disappearing act again and we're talking to her right now. Well, Mom and Dad are yelling, I'm really just listening and trying to blend in to the baseboards. Besides, I have to work this afternoon, eleven to six. Do you want to come over and swim after I get off? You can tell me about the new store."

"Geez, what's the matter with your sister? This is the third time this month, isn't it? Well, okay, how about eight? Great, see you later! Bye!" Laurie said and she hung up.

When Julie came back to the breakfast room Dr. Hathaway had left for work and Mrs. Hathaway was going upstairs. Julie got another bowl of cereal and sat opposite her younger sister.

"So, are you grounded?" she asked and reached for the sugar.

"Yeah," Jo answered, "They said something about going over to Shauna's house without knowing anything about her. Whatever."

"You know they're right, right?"

"Yeah, but it isn't like that! I know her!"

"So, okay, tell me what you do know," Julie said. She took another bite of cereal and then poured herself a cup of coffee.

"Their name is O'Halloran. They moved all the way out from Ireland! They have the coolest accent. They were living in that apartment complex across town for a while, but they just bought the house down the street. Shauna is in my math class. She's so smart! She helped me study for next week's test yesterday. Anyway, her father was in radio news, a host or something back in

19

Ireland, but now he teaches at the university. Irish studies, I think, something like that. Her mom stays at home now that they have moved to the U.S. I don't know what she does, but she used to be in advertising. She makes the best cookies! An old family recipe. You've just got to try them!"

"Well, you certainly know a lot, don't you?" said Julie, "Anything else I should know?"

"Oh yeah!" Jo replied, she got a dreamy look in her eyes, "Shauna has the cutest older brother. He's in your grade, sis. He has dark hair and his eyes are greener than Shauna's."

"Hmm, what's his name? Maybe I do know him," asked Julie. She rinsed her cereal bowl in the sink and placed it in the dishwasher.

"Christopher. Christopher O'Halloran. Great name, huh? He's tall, too. A little taller than Neal, I think."

"That name does sound familiar," said Julie as she tried to recall where she heard that name before, "As a matter of fact, I think Neal mentioned him last night. Yeah… he said they had Physics together. Maybe I'll ask Mom and Dad if I can have a little get-together tonight!"

"Are you going to invite Christopher?" Jo asked with that dreamy look in her eyes again.

"Of course!" said Julie going upstairs.

After Julie got off work that evening she called Neal and asked him if he wanted to swim later. She also mentioned Christopher and asked Neal to invite him, stating that she would like to meet him and welcome him to Riverside.

"Why the sudden interest in Chris, Jules?" asked Neal when he saw through her ruse.

"No reason. I just wondered if he would like to come over. Jo spent the night at their house last night, and she mentioned him. I figured since you two were friends you would want to invite him."

"Sure, I'll ask. What time did you say, Jules? Eight? Okay, see ya then! Bye!"

Christopher was able to come with the stipulation that he was home by ten. When he and Neal arrived at Julie's house David and Laurie were already there.

"Hi, Christopher, right?" Julie inquired, "I'm Julie. Glad you could come! This is Laurie Whitcomb and her boyfriend, David Hawthorne.

"Hi, Chris O'Halloran," he turned to Julie, "Thank you for inviting me." He handed her a plate of Mrs. O'Halloran's famous cream filled Irish lace cookies.

Julie took the plate, sampled a cookie and passed the plate around.

"Thank you," she said, "These are wonderful! You're

going to have to bring more the next time you come!" She smiled as they walked out to the pool.

"I've noticed your accent, Chris." Laurie said, "Where are you from?"

"Claregalway, Ireland. It's a small town with about the same number of people as Carson High, though i'tis growing."

"Wow! What's it like? I've always wanted to visit Ireland," David asked.

"Very different from here. In my town everyone knows everyone else. Ye can't even blow your nose without everyone knowing! I miss that; people here don't interact the same way we do. They stick ta themselves. I've been in Riverside since June and you are the only people willing ta invite me inta your group."

"Hey, anytime," Julie said, "You're always welcome!"

"Thanks!"

"As long as you bring more cookies!"

The group of friends, along with their newest member, enjoyed a fun and relaxing evening at the end of another sweltering day. As the last rays of sunshine began to sink below the horizon and painted the sky glorious shades of purple, pink, red, and orange, the conversation returned to Christopher's past.

"So, where did you say you were from again, Chris?" Julie asked.

"Claregalway. It's a small town off the River Clare just outside of Galway, hence the name. My Da is from there, but when he met and married Ma they moved ta Clifden. Then about five years ago we moved back ta Claregalway. We're Scots-Irish actually. Ma was born and raised in Edinburgh."

"Wow, that's sounds exciting! What's it like there?" David asked, genuinely intrigued.

"Exciting? I don't know if I would say that, but then again, I'm used ta it," Chris laughed but then his eyes got a faraway look in them as he remembered his homeland. "Ah, if only you could see it; the way the breeze from the river sweeps across the grasses, or the smell o' the sea in the air in Clifden, the sound o' the ships in the harbor, and the workers at the docks laughing and joking. I miss my home."

"Sounds beautiful, Chris." Julie said softly. "I would love to see your old home someday. Do you have any pictures or video?"

"Aye, I do in fact. I made sure I took lots of stills before we left. We dinna have much warning, so I was only able ta take one video of Clifden. Perhaps I'll show them t'ye one day."

23

"Oh yes! Please do, Chris! I would like to see them, too," Laurie chimed in.

"Well, alright, next weekend then. We are having a little gathering for my sister, Shauna. It's her birthday, and I honestly would love ta have a reason not ta be there! All her friends seem to have a crush on me... Canna understand little girls..."

"Ah come now, with those dashing green eyes of yours how can anyone resist you!" Neal teased, batting his eyes and making swooning noises much to the amusement of his friends.

"Hush up, ye don't know what it's like!" Chris said, striking a tragic pose.

"Drama geek," Neal said. "Come on, it's almost ten and you promised you'd be home by then."

"Yes, Ma."

"Wow, he's hot!" Laurie said, unabashed, after Neal and Chris left.

"Thanks." David replied dejectedly.

"You're still pretty alright, Dave, but I speak the truth. Chris is hot. Can't deny simple fact."

"Julie, will you please inform my soon-to-be-ex girlfriend about a man's sensitivities when his girl–"

But Julie was a million miles away, thinking about

24

that intriguing young Irishman down the street.

"I wonder how sad he must be," she said. "He didn't seem that way, but sometimes I would catch a look that spoke volumes. Don't you wonder what he had to give up? What he left behind? He said they had to leave in a hurry, I wonder what happened…"

"Earth to Julie! I know that look; don't go getting any ideas. He is not your project." Laurie said and waved her hand in front of Julie's eyes to no avail.

"Come now, aren't you the least bit curious? Think of it, a fairy tale right under our noses!"

With that both Laurie and David knew it was a lost cause to try any further and they went home.

The next morning Julie woke early so she could help her mother with breakfast. Sunday morning breakfast was always a tradition in the Hathaway home, and each member of the family always participated in the preparations. Ever since Julie could remember, Sunday breakfast was the time when the family got together and enjoyed each other's company before church. The meal was always the same, too; home fries, eggs over medium, sausage, biscuits or muffins, coffee, and fresh squeezed orange juice, all from the local Farmer's Market. Things haven't been the same since Julie's older brother Josh left for college last year, but they always left an empty chair for him and called him right before breakfast. Joshua loved those calls and waited eagerly for them each week.

Julie was in charge of making the home fries, one of her favorites. When she walked into the kitchen her father was hard at work mixing the batter for the biscuits and her mother was making the coffee.

"Good morning, ragamuffin!" Her father exclaimed as she entered.

"Good morning, sweetheart," her mother added.

"Morning! Did you sleep well? I did, like a rock. I don't even remember falling asleep." Julie replied and pulled out the cutting board and knife.

"Yes, we did. I washed and peeled the potatoes for you sweetheart. They're all ready."

"Thanks, Mama. That will save time." Julie sliced the potatoes and set them aside so she could start on the onion. When she finished that she pulled out the big frying pan and added oil. Once it heated a little she added the potatoes and onions to the pan and stirred them. A few minutes later Johannah came down the back stairs, rubbing the sleep out of her eyes.

"Hi," she said as she stumbled into a chair and yawned, "I'll get the juice started in a minute, promise."

"My, my, Jo, still asleep?" Julie asked and handed her

26

a glass of water.

"Yeah, a little. I couldn't get to sleep until after one last night. I'm so sleepy!" she yawned.

"That wouldn't have anything to do with the fact that you stayed up late playing video games, would it?" Dr. Hathaway asked with a smile.

"Oh, you know about that, huh? Oops…" Jo answered.

They all laughed and went back to preparing the meal. As Jo made fresh squeezed orange juice in the juicer Dr. Hathaway finished the biscuits. Julie added some paprika to the potatoes, gave them a quick turn, lowered the heat and covered them. Then pulled out another pan and started on the sausage.

"So tell me, Sis, how was your 'get-together'? I was dying to join you, but mama wouldn't let me." Johannah said with a chastised look at their mother.

"Of course not, Jo. You're grounded and that was for your sister. I know how close you two are, but Julie has to have some time alone with her friends."

"Thanks, Mom," Julie laughed and grabbed a chair next to her little sister while she waited on her part of the meal to finish cooking.

"It was a lot of fun, Jo! We just sat around the pool and talked, but that was the best part. Chris told us a little bit about his home in Ireland. They come from a

27

small town, smaller than Riverside, and he misses it a lot. Thank you so much for mentioning him, by the way. He was lonely and sad about the people here not welcoming him, and now he's glad that he has some friends. Say, did you know it was Shauna's birthday next weekend? Chris asked us to go hang out with him and I'm sure the O'Halloran's wouldn't mind if you came, too."

"Yes, I did know, but I didn't know how to ask for permission to go… You know, grounded? So… Mom? Dad? Can I go?" Jo asked with puppy dog eyes and hands clenched in hope.

"No, you are still grounded, Jo." Her mother replied.

"Aw, Mom! Please? It's her birthday!"

"And you're grounded."

"Please? I promise I won't have a good time!"

"Oh really?" Mrs. Hathaway laughed and took the eggs out of the pan. "How will you manage that?"

"No, Jo, I'm afraid this is what being grounded means," their father said. "Give your gift to Julie and she will deliver it for you."

"Alright, but man! It was at that new vintage-style arcade, too!" Johannah sighed.

"Okay everyone," Julie said, "Everything is ready. It's time to call Josh and eat!"

3

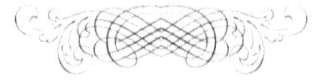

Neal joined Julie and her family at church and sat with them during the service. Neal's family didn't go to church and they didn't believe in God, so one day about ten years ago Julie asked Neal and Laurie to go with her. At first Neal declined, but the next day Laurie and Julie were talking about the new song they learned in Children's Church, "Joshua Fought the Battle of Jericho," and Neal loved the line about the walls coming down. He decided to go the next time and has gone ever since, much to his mother's chagrin. Laurie sang the song for her parents, who remembered singing it when they were children. They decided that they were going to raise their children in church, just as they were, and *they* have been going ever since. All three had accepted Christ together at the age of eight and were baptized together, too. They believed it further sealed them as family for all eternity.

All three friends were in the church drama group and were also part of the church youth group. They helped the music and youth ministers with skits or plays and helped with set design for the Christmas and Easter services. They enjoyed being an active part of the church and were always willing to help when needed.

As the service ended and everyone went back home Julie asked Neal if he thought asking Chris to go with them next week was a good idea.

"Haven't thought about it, Jules," he said. "We never really talked about it before. I have a study session with him tomorrow before our Physics test on Friday, so I'll ask him."

"Would you? Thanks! I make no apologies for being a Christian and he has to know that up front. Otherwise I'll feel like I'm not being honest. With the way folks are nowadays, so full of hatred for Christians, I'd feel better knowing that he knew the truth."

"Don't sweat it. I'm with you on this one. He should

know who we are and what we believe, even if we end up losing him as a friend."

So the next day after classes ended Neal met with Chris in the library and they took a table in the back.

"There's something that both Julie and I think you should know," Neal said after they had been working for a while.

"Oh yeah, what's that?"

"We're Christians. We thought you should know in case you didn't want to be around us anymore."

"Och! Is that all? I thought it was serious! Ye had me worried! That's cool. I figured ye were because ye were both so kind ta me."

"We're that transparent, huh?"

"Aye, but it's good."

"How so?"

"Well, the few Protestants I've met have been rather snobbish ta me, so it was nice ta see people that truly lived out their faith. There was a church back home that I used ta stop in from time ta time. It was run by this sweet old married couple, and ta me, they were true Christians. The people that attended were very different from their pastor and his little old wife, though. They were snobbish, like I said, and they always stared at me like I was an interloper because I was Catholic. They never welcomed me or asked me how I was or ennythin', just stared and scowled. One day, the pastor's wife took me aside and told me not ta think poorly of Protestants because o' what the people did, that it was about the faith. She said one day I would meet people with a real heart for God. So, when I met all of ye I decided she was right."

"So does that mean you're a Christian, too?"

"Eh, not really," he hedged, "I was raised Irish Catholic, but we were never very devout. It was more of a political status for us, aye? Now, my grandparents, hoo, are they devout!" Chris said and whistled as loudly as he could in the library.

Neal laughed and then asked if Chris would like to join them one Sunday.

"Eh, well, I'd have ta think about that, but maybe."

So that's what's wrong with them, Bruce thought as he hid in the back of the library.

He stuffed his textbooks into his bag and walked towards the front of the now-empty library. *Always wondered what made her so different. Guess now I know. Hope she doesn't bring that stuff to me. I don't want none of that Christian stuff!* He stopped at the desk and handed the librarian his homework.

"Not that I mind doing this, Michael. After all, you

have the approval of the school board," Mrs. Mayweather said as she sealed the envelope containing his homework. She stamped the date and time on the seal and dropped it in the inter-office mail slot. She purposely used his first name because she simply refused to condone his new behavior. "But why don't you just turn it in while you're in class? It seems rather silly to come here each afternoon, do all that work, and then not turn it in yourself." She fished around under the desk and produced a similar envelope containing his grades on previous homework assignments.

"Well, see, it's like this, ma'am," Bruce said with a smile as he accepted the envelope. "I got a reputation to maintain. How would it look if I started doing my homework and turning it in? And please call me Bruce, please?" He opened the envelope and peeked at the contents, then added it to his bag.

"Another A?" Mrs. Mayweather asked.

"Of course. School is my ticket outta here," he replied.

"Things have gotten worse at home?" She asked, but Bruce just smiled and ignored the question.

"You know, Michael, I've known you since you were five years old. You used to climb the steps of my back porch and knock on the door until I answered. Remember? I always had fresh cookies for you."

33

"I remember, ma'am." Bruce responded. "They were the best. And it's Bruce now."

She just smiled and continued, "I must say, I don't like this path you've chosen. You're a good kid, kind and considerate. Why this change? Why act like a bully and a tough guy? The offer to come live with me still stands..." she hinted.

"Nah, but thanks Mrs. M. I can handle it. Besides, one more year and I'll be gone. See ya tomorrow."

Bruce heard her sigh as he left the library.

How can I tell her I have to keep people out? He thought. *She can't understand. I have to protect myself; protect her, too. I have to. No one else will.*

When Bruce got home he quietly let himself in the back door and listened intently. *He ain't home, good.* He went upstairs and deposited his books in the closet of his room. He grabbed his guitar and quickly tuned it. He strummed a few bars to warm up, and then started working on his newest song. It was a beautiful ballad with just a hint of Spanish influence. Few would know it, but Bruce was an exceptional guitarist. He could play anything from Irish drinking songs to Spanish lullabies. Sometimes he added his rich baritone voice to the songs, too.

About an hour later he heard his father's clunker coming down the street. *Time to go,* he thought. *From the sound of it I don't want to be here.* He put his guitar carefully away, grabbed his keys, cracked his bedroom window so he could get back in, and locked his bedroom door behind him. He quickly grabbed some food out of the kitchen and left through the back door as his father came in the front. He walked his bike to the end of the block before starting it so his father wouldn't hear.

Now, where shall I go to pass the time? He mused. *Looks like another late night, great.* He decided to go into the city and see what he could find. He turned down 42nd Street and disappeared around a corner just as it started to rain.

Eight o'clock that evening found Bruce in the seedier section of the city outside of a bar and grill that was a college favorite. Bruce and two of his older friends hung around outside watching the people come and go while attempting to stay out of the rain.

"Man, this bites," Jake said. "Let's go someplace else. We've been out here forever."

"Stop saying that, you sound old. No one says 'bites' anymore, bro. Yeah, looks like the place is packed," Matt replied. "What about your sister's place, or yours?"

"Nah, she's home tonight." Jake answered. "And my place is a wreck. Bruce? Let's go to your place."

"My dad's home," Bruce answered. He suddenly found a crack in the pavement very intriguing.

"Man, this bites," Jake said again. "Who else do we know?"

"Listen, I'll catch up with you guys later," Bruce said, pre-occupied. "See ya!"

"Man, this bites," he heard Jake say yet again as he walked to where his bike was parked.

He drove around in the rain for a while and came to the inner city's youth center where Julie worked. He recognized her car in the parking lot, so he pulled in next to it just as she hurried out.

"Hey! Hathaway!" Bruce said and waved.

"What, are you stalking me now?" Julie said and turned to face him.

"Nah, it's not like that! Honest! I was just driving around and saw your car. Don't jump down my throat!"

"Oh, alright," she said and calmed down a little, though still on her guard. "What are you doing out so late? It's after ten."

"Lookin' for somethin' to do. You know, you should ask for better hours. It's late and it's not safe down here. I thought all the kids were sent home by nine anyway."

"They are, but I stay to help set up for the next day. You know, set up the tables, put things away, close down, that kind of thing. It's only on Mondays and Wednesdays anyway, and sometimes weekends." She paused. "Why do you care?" She had a quizzical look on her face.

Now you've done it, Weber. She thinks you're up to something.

"Just not safe is all. I don't like seeing women get hurt, okay?" he mumbled.

"Well, I'll be fine. I study martial arts here, too," Julie answered. "I'm a pretty good fighter when I have to be." She opened her car door and got in.

"Really? Well, good," Bruce said. "I'll see you later." He stayed long enough to make sure she was okay then drove off.

Hmmm, wonder what discipline she studies...

He shut down the motor at the end of the block and wheeled his bike into his driveway. He climbed onto the roof via the tree in the backyard, then swung out to catch the ledge under his window. He quietly opened the window further and snuck inside. Securing the window behind him, he listened for his father.

He's still awake. Good thing I came in through the window.

Suddenly his father let out a string of expletives and Bruce heard a bottle shatter against the wall.

Another lovely day in the Weber household. He thought as he quietly prepared for bed. *One more year...*

Bruce woke early the next morning and found his father snoring on the sofa, deep in a drunken slumber. There were also several empty cans of alcohol scattered around and broken glass in the corner. *I'll clean that up after school. I hate living in a mess.* Bruce quietly fixed a bowl of cereal and took it outside to eat. It had started raining again sometime during the night and continued on till morning. Bruce watched the puddles forming in the yard. For this one moment he was at peace, everything was calm, and he could breathe again; even if only for a moment.

Things weren't always this way, and as he listened to the rain he remembered how things used to be:

I remember when Dad built that treehouse for me and Tom. It was so much fun watching him put it together all wrong and getting frustrated. Mom came out with the instructions but Dad refused to read them.

"I can do it just fine without instructions," he said, "It can't be that hard!"

Of course, eventually he gave in and read them. Turns out he was trying to build it upside down! That was so much fun. Tom just rolled on the ground laughing. We used to have a lot of times like that. Man, Tom and I played in that treehouse for years. Climbing up and down, walking on top, reaching to see who could grab the highest branch. Even when we fell we still got back up there. How many times did we break bones? Bah, I can't remember. Oh well, it was fun!

Then we grew up. We started playing football back here. Dad loved to play with us, Mom too. We would team up and play for hours on the weekends. Tom and I would take those two trees over there as the end zone, Mom and Dad would take the house and the fence as theirs. Mom was good, never could score on her.

When did it all start to fall apart? Was it before or after Tom was killed..?

I think it was just before. Dad was laid off from work and couldn't find another job. Mom kept telling him it would be alright, they could make it just fine on her salary, but Dad wouldn't hear of it. He was the man of the house, he said, and it was his responsibility.

Tom had just started his senior year and was hoping to get a good scholarship so he could go to college. He started working in the city to help pay for things around here. I was still in junior high then. Tom said he hated his job but it paid well so he kept going. Mom didn't like it either, said they kept him out too late, especially on the weekends when all the drunks were out driving around.

Then one night Tom never made it back.

That was the worst night of my life. Or so I thought. I can still hear Mom's scream when she answered the door and the police were there to tell her that her son was killed by a drunk driver. She crumpled to the floor as I ran downstairs. Dad just stood there. He didn't say anything, didn't do anything, just stood there. Frozen. Stone.

They said Tom was so badly injured that we couldn't see him. They said he might have lived if he hadn't been on a motorcycle at the time. How do you like that? He might still be here if I hadn't convinced him to buy that bike. My bike now.

Yeah, that's when Dad started drinking. He finally did find a job, though, in the city, working in the courthouse. He hates it, I can tell, but he still goes. Every day. Never searched for another job. He just drowned himself in booze. Mom hated that. She hated the fact that her husband drank so heavily when that was what killed her son. I think maybe that's what changed Dad. He knew he had lost her respect.

That's when the fighting started.

Man, those were some bad fights. I wasn't here for the beginning of it all. The folks sent me to that special school for kids dealing with major issues. But I came back. Wrong time, too. Yeah, those were some really bad fights. As soon as I was old enough I learned how to drive so I didn't have to be here. I fixed up Tom's bike and drove away from it all. Mom hated me for that, driving Tom's bike. Driving a motorcycle at all. That's what killed her son. She hated me for that. She hated Dad for drinking. She hated us, so she left. No goodbyes, no letters, no phone calls, she just left.

She left me here with him.

That's when the hitting started.

Bruce realized he was just wasting time and he needed to leave for school. He snuck back inside and rinsed his bowl in the sink. He went upstairs and grabbed his bag, then prepared for school. His father was still snoring on the sofa. He woke him so he wouldn't be late for work before heading outside.

Another lovely day in the Weber household…

4

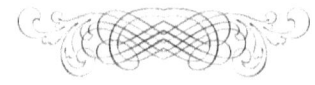

Bruce was in a bad mood by the time he entered the school building that day. He wore a face that told everyone to stay at least ten feet away from him as he walked down the hallways. Solidly built at six foot two and 225 pounds, they were more than happy to oblige. *Good, at least I won't have to talk to anyone.* Everyone scampered to get out of his way and gave him a wide berth. At least, until Julie waved to him from down the hall. *That's unexpected. Why'd she do that?* He nodded to her as he walked into his first classroom of the day. *Hope she doesn't think I've gone soft now that I told*

her I was worried for her last night. Crap, hope that doesn't get around.

Julie stopped by his classroom and dropped a note on his desk, that was all, just dropped off the note and left. He opened the note and read it, "Hi Bruce. Thanks for checking on me last night. That was really sweet. I know it's a dangerous area at night, so I promise to be more careful. I will only have to work nights until Thanksgiving. The center closes its doors then, so I will have to find another job. I feel terrible for all those kids that depend on the center. Anyway, thanks again! Julie." *Great, now she's got ideas.* His fuming rose to a whole new level. *How are you gonna get yourself outta this one, Weber? Can't let this get out or your rep is history. Man, try to do something nice for someone...*

The bell rang to signal classes had begun, but Bruce didn't notice. He was too busy trying to sort out what Julie intended by her message. *What if she starts talking to me? Would that be so bad? Yes, it would be. I can't let anyone get too close. I can't let anyone see how things are. But, maybe it would be ok... No, she could never accept someone as messed up as me. Doesn't matter how much I like her, I can't let her know.* The problem was how will he prevent it? He couldn't very well tell her to stay away. It was too late for that now. He also couldn't let her

43

continue to talk to him. What if his father found out and hurt her? Bruce would never forgive himself if that happened. *I've lost too many people and I'm not about to lose any more.*

He tried to focus on the lecture without appearing to pay attention, not an easy task and certainly made more difficult by his distraction. Eventually the class ended and he made his way to the next one. He shared this class with Neal and wasn't looking forward to the encounter. *What if she told him? They are best friends.* His fears were for naught and the class ended without incident.

Somehow Bruce made it through the day, although if one were to ask him what he learned he wouldn't be able to answer. He started his bike and drove through the parking lot towards the north exit. As he pulled onto the main road away from the school he passed Julie who waited to turn in the opposite direction. She waved again and gave him the warmest smile he had ever received from her. *Great. Now you're really in for it, Weber.* He ignored her and focused on the drive home.

When he entered the house he knew his father wasn't home yet, so he cleaned up the mess from last night. He also got the mail and sorted it. There was a letter in the pile for him from the local university. They were interested in his academic performance and wanted to meet with him to discuss his options. He ran the letter through the shredder and went upstairs. He unlocked his door and flopped down on the bed. *Sorry guys, but you are way too close to home.*

Eventually he got up and went downstairs to finish cleaning before his father came home. He was just about done when he heard his dad's car down the street. He went back upstairs and locked his bedroom door. It was pouring down rain again and he didn't really want to spend the evening driving around in it, so he turned out the light and pretended he wasn't home. He heard his father cursing below at the fact that there was never anything to eat in the refrigerator. He heard a can open and assumed his father started his binge for the night. *Guess it's time to go shopping. Why can't he just do it himself, he buys enough booze? I'm tired of always cleaning up after him. One more year...*

Sometime during the night his father came upstairs and banged wildly on Bruce's door. Bruce pulled the covers higher over his head and if he was a praying man he would have prayed that his father would just leave him alone...

Wednesday night Bruce again went to the youth center and waited for Julie to leave. *What am I doing*

45

here? She already thinks I'm softening up, why am I giving her more ammo? This girl is going to be my undoing. I held out for years, but this year she's going to get me. And still he waited.

When she finally came out a little after ten-thirty she looked up and saw him parked a few feet away.

"What are you doing here tonight, hmm?" Julie asked.

"To be honest, I don't know. Just thought I should be here when you got off."

"Well, thank you. And don't think you can get away with not saying hi to me anymore." Julie smiled as she got into her car. She started the engine, waved, and drove away.

Great, now she's got even more ideas. What is it about this girl that makes me do stupid things? And why isn't she afraid of me anymore? That's a better question... Have I lost my edge? Maybe I should start being a jerk again.

He contemplated these thoughts as he drove home.

When Bruce arrived home a little after six-thirty the next day after doing the grocery shopping, his father was not there. Bruce decided to prepare dinner just in case he came home later than usual; if he ever came home at all that night. Sometimes his dad stayed out until a few hours before he needed to leave for work the next morning, and sometimes not at all. Bruce just didn't understand it, but he grabbed the ground pork from the fridge and started frying it for his father's dinner anyway. He pulled the brown sugar, tomato sauce, herbs, and spices from the pantry and started heating the pork while he chopped the peppers and onions. He added these to the ground pork and cooked them until the meat was done and the onions were translucent. He combined the other ingredients into a sauce and then he added the sauce mixture to the pan. He warmed some hamburger buns in the microwave and made himself a Sloppy Joe sandwich for dinner, his own secret recipe. Once he had his fill he set the rest aside until it cooled enough to put in the fridge. His dad hated reheated food, but it was better than nothing.

After dinner Bruce cleaned up the kitchen and went upstairs. It was his laundry night so he started a load and then picked up his guitar. After quickly tuning it he started working on his ballad again, but something wasn't quite right.

"Maybe if I change the key..." he thought aloud. He lowered the key and started from the beginning, this time in B-flat minor.

"Yeah... that's it... that's better. Fits my mood now." Bruce said as he continued to the point where he stopped writing last time.

He started to hum along with his strumming until he developed a complimentary melody for his new song. Every so often he would stop and notate what he had just composed on the sheets of staff paper he kept with his guitar. When he felt he had a solid piece he booted up his laptop and recorded it, just the guitar, so he could work on the lyrics while the music looped in the background. After a few tries he had a good enough version recorded so he set his guitar aside and started contemplating lyrics as he transferred the clothes to the dryer.

"Now, what should this song say...?" He tossed some ideas into the air to see what stuck and decided this one would be a song about loss. The minor key worked perfectly for the lyrics that started flowing from his mind to the paper and when he was finished he picked up the guitar again and sang the entire piece from the beginning.

It was about that time that the clothes were dry and he had to stop to put them away. Just as he was finished and went back to his room he heard his father pull into the driveway. His dad slammed the car door, which apparently didn't close correctly, because his father cursed and kicked it closed. Then he heard him stomp up the front porch stairs and throw open the door, slamming it closed as well. Bruce quickly put his gear away, locked his door and snuck out the window. His heard his dad curse about having to reheat his dinner as he lowered his window to a crack so he could get back in later.

Another lovely day in the Weber household, he thought as he wheeled his bike down the street. *Will things ever change?*

Julie locked her car and entered her house through the garage at about the same time. She had just returned from a study session in Calculus and was starving. She set her things in the breakfast room chair and opened the pantry, looking for a quick snack. She pulled out the tortilla chips and went to the refrigerator for the salsa. She noticed a note addressed to her stuck to the door with a magnet, so she pulled it down and opened it. *Yes! Thanks, Mom, you're the best!* She opened the fridge and there was the dinner her mother left for her on the second shelf, just as the note said. She peeked under the tin foil and saw that it was her favorite, Dijon Chicken. She loved the flavor the Dijon mustard sauce added to the noodles and chicken breast, and it was always better reheated. She placed the plate on the counter to bring it to room temperature before she heated it in the microwave. Meanwhile, she grabbed the salsa and ate just a few chips while she waited.

What an interesting week, she thought to herself. First, she learned that Chris didn't mind at all that they were Christians and even promised to consider going to church with them one day. She recalled Neal's conversation with him and how the people treated Chris back in Ireland. *I guess there's prejudice everywhere, even in the church. How sad.* She tried to remember if she was ever treated that way, but couldn't think of a time. *Unless you count my very first time at youth group... that was hard.*

She remembered sitting all by herself that night because Neal and Laurie were both busy. They had been looking forward to being old enough to join the youth group and when they finally were it was only Julie that went. She thought about not going at all, but her friends insisted that she go and tell them all about it. She remembered sitting towards the front by the stage and seeing some people she knew from school. They were all a few years older than her, but she thought they would still be sociable. Instead they smiled at her and then promptly shouldered her back out of their discussion. Julie was devastated. She was so hurt that Christians would treat her that way. Weren't they supposed to be welcoming and kind?

She moved to the back of the room and stayed in the shadows during the meeting until her Mom came to pick her up. When she told her mother about what happened she started crying. Her mom laid Julie's head down in her lap and stroked her hair while Julie cried. When the tears were spent she told Julie that she was sure the kids didn't mean to hurt her. They probably assumed that she was just passing by and said hello, and if they had known she was there by herself they would have included her. Julie didn't think that was true, but it did make a small amount of sense. She considered the fact that they were all friends before she came and maybe that was all there was to it; that it didn't occur to them to include her. She decided to try again the next week and she had much better success. Her mom was right, it wasn't intentional.

Maybe it was like that for Chris. Maybe he didn't have anyone to tell him except that old lady. Perhaps I can approach him from that angle... A shared experience goes a long way... She got up and reheated her food in the microwave. She put away the chips and salsa and poured a glass of raspberry iced tea. While she waited for her dinner to heat she went back over the events of the past week.

Let's see, next was that strange encounter with Bruce! Talk about weird! He just showed up at work, like he'd

51

planned it. But it did make me stop and think…

She was so surprised to see him sitting on his bike next to her car. At first she was afraid. After all, he had been rude to her for years, but he made no intimidating moves. She thought she would really be in trouble then, with no one to help her if he should try anything. But he didn't. In fact, he said he was worried about her. Well, not in so many words, but still… *He even stayed until I was safely in my car…* That really surprised her. Bruce used to be like that, kind and helpful. But that was back when they were kids, when he went by his first name. *I'd forgotten about that! He changed right after his brother died. Guess that would really change someone. I don't know what I'd do if anything ever happened to Jo or Josh.* The thought alone made her shiver and she was glad when the microwave chimed. She got her plate and glass and went to the table to eat. She said grace and then dug in with gusto. After all, it was her favorite meal.

Once she finished eating she rinsed her plate and checked the dishwasher to see if there were clean or dirty dishes inside. They were dirty so she added her plate, glass, and fork. It was full so she started it, and then went to the family room to watch some TV before going upstairs. She thought again about Bruce and his sudden change. *I decided to run my own little experiment and wrote that note. Boy was he surprised! But he didn't make a scene or throw it back in my face. Maybe he's softening towards me. Maybe I really can help him and be a friend. Maybe that's all he needs...* She was startled but not afraid when he showed up at the youth center again the next day. She made a genuine effort to be a friend and let him know she appreciated his concern. *He just thought he should be there. And he tries to be so tough. I wonder what ever happened to his mom. I haven't seen her around town in a long time. He did mention not wanting to see women get hurt... I hope nothing happened to her! Is that what changed him? Could there be something really wrong? Lord, are you trying to tell me to be a friend to Bruce? Is he ready? Am I the one that You sent to him? Help me help him, Lord. Give me the right words to say.* She turned off the television and went upstairs. As she passed her sister's room she knocked on the door. There was no answer, so she peeked inside. The lights were off and Jo was asleep. *She turned in early. I should have been quieter, hope I didn't wake her.* Julie softly closed the door and went to her own room to prepare for bed. She knew from the note that her dad was at the hospital and her mom was working late, but would be in around ten. Julie waited until she heard her mom pull into the garage and then went to sleep.

53

Julie awoke to frantic knocking at her door. She glanced at the clock and noted that it was almost two in the morning. She looked over at her door as her parents opened it, obviously very upset.

"What's wrong?" she asked as she turned on the light. "What happened?"

"Did you tell Jo she could go out? She's still grounded." Her father asked, clearly agitated.

"No, of course not. I know she's still... wait... she isn't here?" Julie was wide-awake and bounded out of bed. She raced down the hall towards her sister's room.

"I checked on her before I went to bed. She was in her room sound asleep!" She called over her shoulder as she opened Jo's door. The bed looked too lumpy to be Jo's slight frame and with the light on she noticed that it was also too long. She threw back the covers and there were the two pillows Jo slept with as well as one of her collectible teddy bears. Julie turned around, wide-eyed, and looked at her parents who were standing in the doorway.

"We came to check on her before turning in and immediately knew that was not her in that bed. Did you see her at all after you came home?" Her mother asked, her arms akimbo, and a frown on her face.

"No, honestly Mom. I just peeked inside and thought she was asleep in bed. I didn't want to bother her so I just kept going. I'm sorry, I should have checked, or woke her up, or something. I just didn't think she would leave when she knew she was grounded."

"I'm sorry, Julie. It isn't your fault and I'm not angry with you at all. I *am* angry with your sister, though, and extremely disappointed in her." Her mother said. She turned off the light and all three went back downstairs to start calling Jo's friends. As they got to the bottom of the stairs they heard a noise upstairs and as if they all had the same thought, turned and quietly went back upstairs, Dr. Hathaway in the lead.

They waited outside Jo's door and heard another sound, like a window being lowered. Julie threw open the door and turned on the light. There was Jo, tiptoeing over to her bed.

"Busted!" Julie said and let her parents take over.

5

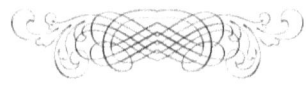

Julie tried to go back to sleep, but was unable. She just couldn't understand what had gotten into her sister. Jo was a good kid. There was no reason whatsoever for her to wander off or sneak out. *Unless... she could be hanging out with the wrong crowd... No way, not my sister! She knows better!* But Julie couldn't shake the feeling that she didn't know her little sister anymore.

The next morning she slipped off quietly to school. It was Friday, her light day. She had signed up for a study hour and student aiding on Fridays and now she was glad she did. However, the lack of sleep was really getting to her as the day passed. She was able to do most of her homework and even some light reading during her study hour, and the teacher she was aiding for did not need her help that day. She asked for a pass to go to the library instead, which the teacher gladly supplied. She found a quiet spot in the back of the library where students normally didn't go and settled into one of the soft armchairs. She placed her bags next to her, but as she did one of the books slipped out. As she reached for it she saw a familiar pair of combat boots and torn jeans against the wall. She raised her head and peeked through the shelves. Sure enough, there was Bruce sitting against the wall with a pad of paper and a textbook. Julie was contemplating approaching him when he spoke.

"Don't say a word to anyone, got it?" He kept his eyes on his paper and continued writing as if he hadn't spoken.

"Sure... No problem... I won't say anything. Are you working on the English assignment? If so, I could really use your help understanding what Ms. Lynn is asking us to do."

"What do you mean? You don't get it?" Bruce finally looked up and faced her.

"No, I don't. Sorry. I didn't get much sleep and

57

couldn't focus in class today."

"I know the feeling. It seems I never get much sleep anymore." He paused and his eyes lost focus for a moment, then he continued, "She's just asking us to rewrite Act II Scene I in our own voice. You know, how we would interpret it or how we would say it today. I think she just wants to see if we understand what Shakespeare was trying to say, that's all."

"Oh, okay. That makes sense! Thank you!" Julie said softly with a smile and went back to her studies.

After a few minutes Bruce asked, "Why didn't you get much sleep? Partying too much?"

"Hardly! That would at least be believable. My sister snuck out last night."

"So? What's so bad about that?"

"What's so bad? She's only eleven! She shouldn't be out wandering around by herself, especially late at night. She didn't come home until after two o'clock this morning!"

"Shhh!" someone said, so Julie grabbed her purse and went to where Bruce was sitting against the wall.

"Who said you could sit here?" he asked.

"Oh hush, Bruce. You can't fool me anymore, so don't even try it." She smiled when she said it, but Bruce also knew she meant it.

58

"You're infuriating," he muttered.

"Thank you! I do try!" Julie replied with a wink and a smile.

"Eleven, huh? Yeah, that's really young. Does she do that often?" he asked as she settled in.

"Unfortunately, yes. I don't know what's gotten into her. I think she's hanging out with a bad crowd. This kind of behavior started about six months ago, maybe a little longer... I can't get through to her, but I keep trying to be a good example. I just don't get it..."

Bruce was quiet for a moment, then turned to her and said, "I'll see what I can find out. Remember not to tell anyone you saw me in here. I got a reputation to maintain." He gathered his books and stood up.

Julie also stood up and asked, "I won't say anything, but at least tell me why the secrecy? Why hide back here and try to do your homework?"

"You wouldn't understand. I gotta go. And Hathaway, don't think this makes us friends." He walked away.

"Sure, right, uh-huh, in your dreams buddy." She said to herself quietly as she went back to her spot.

He'll see what he can do? Wonder what he meant by that... He does hang out with a bad crowd himself... maybe...

Julie could no longer focus on her studies so she sat

59

for the last few minutes of the school day and thought about her sister.

When she got home that afternoon there was a note for her on the fridge, which simply said to call Mom, and so dialed her mother's agency.

"Hi Mom," she said when Cynthia picked up the line.

"Hi, sweetie, listen," she said, "I need you to come pick up Johannah and take her home. She is not to be out of your sight for a single second. Do you understand?"

"Well, no not really. Why? I was planning on hanging out with Laurie tonight."

"I'm sorry, but we can't trust Jo to do as she's told. I left work today to pick her up from school and bring her here. Your father spent the entire night camped outside her bedroom with the door open so she couldn't sneak off again. We just don't know what else to do except put her under house arrest with constant supervision. She's helping Maria with the filing right now, just to keep her busy and supervised, but I have a meeting and I can't let her stay here all day. Please come pick her up and keep her with you until I get home?"

"Wow, yeah sure, Mom. It's ok. I'm on my way, I just have to call Laurie first and see if she would mind Jo tagging along or if she just wants to come here instead.

And Mom, I'm really sorry."

"What on earth for, Julie? This isn't your fault."

"Yes, it is. I should have been a better role model for her. Spent more time with her, or—"

"Julianne Marie Hathaway you stop that this minute! Have you been thinking this all day? You are a *wonderful* sister and this is in no way your fault! Don't you dare blame yourself. Your sister is old enough to know better and the blame rests on her shoulders, not yours. I have to go, but Jo is up front with Maria. I love you, honey, and don't blame yourself."

"Ok, Mom. Bye!" But Julie was far from feeling innocent.

Laurie went with Julie to pick up Jo, but the ride back to the house was quiet.

Jo stormed out of the car and into the house. She raced upstairs and slammed the door. Her father had taken the television and video game system out earlier that day and also moved the tall dresser in front of the window. There was nothing for her to do except homework or reading. The Hathaway's hoped it would serve as a constant reminder to her to be obedient.

Julie climbed the stairs after her sister and opened the door again. She dreaded the argument that would erupt once she did, but Jo didn't say anything. She just laid on the bed with her arms crossed, a scowl on her face. Laurie and Julie decided to hang out in Josh's room which was across the hall from Jo so they could keep an eye on her. They also decided it was the perfect time to do their homework, so they sat at the desk and the edge of the bed with their assignments spread out in front of them. Julie had already done much of it earlier that day, so she helped Laurie catch up to her.

"So, guess who I saw coming out of the *library* of all places!" Laurie said during one of their breaks.

"I can't imagine." Julie said, which wasn't a lie, she didn't have to imagine, she knew.

"Bruce! Wonder what he was doing in there, huh?"

"Not really, maybe he was returning a book he borrowed years ago or something. Listen, can I ask you something?" Julie said in the hope of steering the conversation away from Bruce so she could keep her promise.

"Sure, shoot."

"Am I a good person?"

"Whoa, blindsided by my best friend! Where did that come from?" Laurie stopped doodling and stared at Julie as if she'd lost her mind.

In response Julie just looked over to Jo's room and

then back to Laurie.

"Ah, I see. Do you blame yourself for what Jo does?" Laurie said it a little too loudly on purpose; she was hoping Jo was listening to this exchange.

Julie put a finger to her lips in an attempt to quiet Laurie. "I don't exactly blame myself, she knows better, but..."

"But you still think you failed her in some way, right? I know you Julie, you're the world's big sister and you think you have to solve every problem, but you don't. Some things are just bigger than you. This is one of them. It isn't your fault, so stop it."

"I don't try to solve *every* problem, Laurie, just the ones I've caused. I know I failed her in some small way, maybe years ago, and now this really is my fault. I'm asking you to help me figure out what I did wrong."

"You didn't do anything wrong! Stop this, Julie, it isn't healthy! Jo made her choices and now she has to live with them. You have only ever been a great sister, especially to me, and I will not have you talking like this ever again. Now, let's get back to work." Laurie had turned red because she was so angry. Not because she was angry with Julie, but because she was angry with the way Jo caused her best friend to feel. Laurie was very protective of Julie when she got this way. She knew how it ate at her friend like a virus and how Julie would slip further and further into herself until she broke down. She really hoped Jo heard the conversation and was in there thinking about her behavior.

But Jo slipped out somewhere between Julie asking what she did wrong and Laurie saying it was all Jo's fault. As the tears fell from her eyes she left the house and ran down to the new vintage-style arcade. No one understood her, they all thought she was a problem child and irredeemable. She would show them. She would show them all.

As Bruce stopped at a traffic light down the street from the arcade a young girl came rushing past him, wiping her face as if she'd been crying. *Yeah, kid, I know the feeling. Hate to tell ya this, but it doesn't get better. It just gets worse, it always gets worse.* He wore his sunglasses even though the sun was setting. He wasn't ready to let anyone see his newest black eye until he came up with a plausible story, or better yet, until he got into a real fight and could blame it on "the other guy" instead.

This time his father didn't wait until he was drunk to start in on Bruce. He just did. For no reason at all, unless having to reheat the spaghetti counted as a valid reason.

Bruce could still hear his father's voice in his ear: *"You worthless piece of –! What good are you? Can't you even have dinner warm and ready when I come home! No, you run out of here as if my house isn't good enough for you! Got somewhere else you wanna be, huh? Worthless waste of my time!"* Bruce cringed at that moment because that was when he got the black eye. Backhanded in a flash.

Yeah, worthless, that's what I am. Irredeemable. For now. But I'll show you, Dad. I'll show everyone. I'm not a lost cause. I'll make myself filthy rich and show all of you! He started his bike and went in search of some action.

Julie got up a little while later to ask Jo if she was ready for dinner.

"Not again!" she cried and ran around the house looking for her sister.

Laurie came running behind her and asked what happened.

"She's gone! She's gone again! This is all my fault! I was supposed to watch her and I failed!" She grabbed her car keys, but Laurie took them from her.

"I'll drive," she said, "you aren't in any condition to drive right now. Call your mom and tell her what happened. We'll find her, Julie, don't worry. She couldn't have gone far."

They got in Julie's car and drove around town in search of the recalcitrant girl. They stopped at a traffic light near the arcade, which was not in a good location, and saw Bruce next to them. Julie rolled down the passenger window and called out to him.

"Bruce? Jo is missing again, have you seen her?" she looked at him closely and gasped. "What happened? Are you alright?"

"Got in a fight, it's nothing. Is she about this tall with light red hair? She just went in there." And he drove off.

Laurie pulled the car into the parking lot of the arcade and they got out. They found Jo playing with a group of older kids at the skeeball machines. As soon as Jo saw them she turned to her friends and waved goodbye, then ran to intercept Laurie and Julie.

"Let's just go," she said and walked out the door.

Julie was beside herself and simply started crying as she walked out to her car. Laurie dropped them both off and gave Julie the car keys. Mrs. Hathaway had come home while they were out and Dr. Hathaway was on his way. Laurie gathered her books, gave Julie a quick hug, and left out the back door.

Julie called to her outside and apologized for the evening, but Laurie wouldn't hear of it.

"Not your fault, Julie. It isn't. Don't you dare. Don't

you dare! Listen, come over to my house tonight and let your parents handle this. You need to get away and you certainly don't need to be alone right now. Besides," Laurie said with a chuckle, "tomorrow is Chris's sister's birthday and we promised to rescue him from the attack of the little girls. We can go together."

"Sorry, Laur, I can't even think about going after this. Please tell everyone I can't be there and apologize for me. I'll see ya later." Julie turned, dejected, and walked back into the house.

6

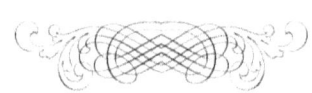

$\mathcal{N}$eal wondered what was wrong as he peeked out his bedroom window, which faced the Hathaway house. He saw Laurie and Julie standing in the backyard and watched as Julie went back into the house, shoulders drawn and head down.

Laurie looked up at that moment and caught his eye. She pointed to the retreating Julie and shook her head slowly side to side. Neal held up one finger then pointed down to his back door. Laurie nodded and started walking over to his house as he went down the back stairs. When he got outside Laurie was standing between the houses so he went over to her and said hello.

"I'll walk you home," he said.

"Thanks," she replied.

When they were out of earshot of both houses Neal asked, "So, it's happening again, huh?"

"Yeah. Jo keeps wandering off even though she knows she's grounded. Julie blames herself. She thinks she failed as a sister, Neal! I think it's really bad this time. Really bad. She wasn't even listening to me at all! I mean, she gets this way sometimes, just really depressed and inward-focused, but this time it's her sister. I think this is more than we can handle..." Laurie was really worried by the time they reached her house.

"Then we'll seek a Higher Power to help us." Neal took her hand and right there in Laurie's driveway they prayed for their best friend.

Several weeks passed and Julie pulled further and further away from her friends. She didn't talk to them after school or between classes; she always slipped into her classroom and buried her face in a book to avoid conversation. People noticed the change in her, but didn't know what to do. Her teachers tried talking to her, her classmates asked if anything was wrong, and her parents tried coaxing her to talk. Nothing worked.

Neal, Chris, and Laurie were really worried about her and decided to pay her a visit one Friday after school. As a group they decided an intervention was the best they could do for their friend, and they weren't going to leave until they reached her.

"So, we just show up and what? Tie ourselves ta her house?" Chris asked. He had never actually done an intervention before and wasn't sure what to do.

Neal laughed, "No, we just sit her down and be supportive until she opens up. You know, get her to talk to us, get it out of her system, and such."

"Ah, I see. And this'll work?"

"Maybe, maybe not. But we won't know until we try." Laurie responded to his question and tried to sound optimistic but she had her doubts as well.

They were sitting around one of the study tables in the library after school planning their intervention. They tossed around a few ideas, but just sitting with her seemed to be the best of the bunch.

"This may sound crazy, but why are we doing this? I mean, I know she's down and all, but why is this a bad thing? People get sad from time to time, I know I do, but I always perk up again. Are ye afraid she won't?" Chris asked.

"That's right; you haven't been through one of these! I'm sorry, Chris. You fit right in with us and I sometimes forget that you're new here," Neal said. "Julie has these pet projects. She loves to tackle the world's problems. Doesn't matter what kind, she has to try to fix things. If someone is sad, she *has* to cheer them up. If someone is hurt, she *has* to heal them. If ever anyone was in need she's there. It's a great quality to have, but sometimes she goes too far."

"We've known her since we were all babies and she has always been the world's big sister. She genuinely wants to help everyone, and she doesn't understand that sometimes problems can't be solved; you just have to live with them. Well, this is one of those times. You know about her sister, right?" Laurie asked.

"I know *of* her. She's *my* sister's friend, remember? What did she do? Is she alright? We haven't seen her for a while."

"That depends on your definition of 'alright' actually..." Neal replied. "You see, Johannah has this habit of doing whatever she wants without regard to anyone. She gets an idea in her head and acts on it. It hasn't been a big deal until recently. Mostly she would just make little mistakes or misjudgments, but about seven months or so ago she started wandering off

71

without telling anyone where she was. The first few times her parents were so worried they were calling the police and the morgue! Jo didn't really seem to understand what was wrong and so she kept doing it. She claimed to leave notes, or that she tried to call, but I don't really think she tried all that hard. She has this rebellious streak in her that wasn't there before."

"Wow, that's news ta me! Is she a bad kid? Should I be worried about my sister? Dinna be angry! I have ta ask!" Chris held his hands up apologetically.

"It's okay, we understand," Laurie said. "And Jo is a good kid, so I don't think you should be worried. Yet. I think Jo's found some new friends that are leading her down the wrong path, but Julie blames herself. She listens to the voices in her head telling her that she's a screw up and a failure. She just stops hearing anything else."

"Right, and our job is to help Julie see that and *stop* blaming herself." Neal added.

"That's a lot ta take on..." Chris said and looked away from them for a moment.

Laurie and Neal glanced at each other. They never thought that Chris wouldn't want to help. Neal was just about to say he didn't have to when Chris clapped his hands and stood up.

"So let's get started!" he said and picked up his bag.

Bruce sat in his usual spot in the library and wondered why these people always picked *that* table to sit around and talk. Now he had way more information than he wanted. *Not your problem, Weber. Just go home and let them handle it.* But he couldn't stop wondering if Julie was really going to be okay.

When Chris, Laurie, and Neal arrived at Julie's house a few minutes later they could hear an argument going on inside. They hesitated before knocking, but decided to go ahead with their plan; maybe Julie needed a reason to leave.

When Julie answered the door they heard Jo yelling at her parent's upstairs.

"Sorry guys, now is a bad time," she said.

"We know. We thought maybe you wanted to take a walk and let them handle your sister," Laurie said with a smile. "C'mon, we'll take a walk."

"No, but thank you. I should stay here and help them."

"Nothing doing, Jules. We won't go far, just down the street, so they can call if they need you. We aren't leaving without you." Neal poured support and understanding into his gaze and hoped she understood he was only trying to help her.

"Maybe just a few minutes then…" Julie shut the door, but came back after a moment with her sweater and keys. She locked the front door and went with her friends down the street.

"Listen, I know you guys are worried about me, but I really don't need this intervention. I just have to figure out what I did wrong and fix it."

"So, you figured us out, huh? Well, you do need it, Julie. You need to understand Jo's behavior isn't your fault." Laurie stopped and held Julie's arm. She implored her to understand that sometimes people really do make their own decisions and it had nothing to do with her.

"You don't understand, Laurie. The argument you walked in on was my parents telling Jo they were sending her off to live with our grandparents in Sioux Falls at the end of the semester. She completely ignored her grounding and went off twice after the night you came over. She keeps going to that gaming center and hanging out with those freshmen we saw. When did she even meet them? I should have paid more attention to her. Then this wouldn't have happened and they wouldn't be sending her away!" Julie cried and took off down the street back to her house.

They ran after her, but she was faster and closed the

door just as they got there. They knocked several times, but Julie wouldn't answer.

About thirty minutes later the arguing stopped, but Julie was still lying on her bed crying.

This is all my fault! Why couldn't I have paid more attention to Jo, or noticed her new friends sooner! Now they're sending my baby sister away and there's nothing I can do! I spent so much time working on everyone else's problems that I wasn't there for her when she needed me. What am I going to do...?

She mulled over these thoughts for hours and finally fell into an agitated sleep.

She awoke around two in the morning to the sound of crying from her sister's room. Julie had fallen asleep in her clothes so she changed into pajamas. She threw her robe around her shoulders and walked softly down the hall. She stopped to listen at her sister's door.

"Jo?" Julie said as she tapped lightly on the door.

"Just go away!" Jo said. "I don't want to talk to you!"

Julie started to walk away, but then stopped and turned around. She opened the door and walked in.

"Tough! You are going to talk to me. Or at least just listen..."

"Argh! Doesn't anyone care about what *I* want!?"

They were keeping their voices down, but Julie could still hear the passion in her sister's plea. She sat down on the edge of the bed and gathered her thoughts.

"Listen, Jo. I'm really sorry that I haven't been a good sister to you. I just want you to know that—"

"What!? What nonsense are you spouting now?" Jo sat up and stared at her sister in the dark room.

"I'm serious, Jo. I've been thinking about this for weeks and I finally realized that if I had been a better sister to you then you wouldn't need to act this way. If I had paid more attention to you then Mom and Dad wouldn't send you away. I wasn't there for you and I'm sorry, but I will be from now on. Promise."

"Are you really sitting there thinking this is about you? It has nothing to do with *you!* You don't understand. You can't! Just go away and leave me alone! Go on! Get out!" Jo threw one of her pillows at her and turned away to face the wall. Julie sat there for a minute and finally decided it was best to go back to her room.

Now what have I done? Have I just made things worse? Was I too late? What did she mean by I can't understand? She's my sister! We've always been so close. I must have really messed up this time. Julie tossed and turned the rest of the night but sleep eluded her.

ca

76

Bruce tossed and turned but sleep eluded him as well. Every time he closed his eyes he saw Julie with tears in her eyes staring down at her dead sister.

If I'd known that girl was Julie's sister I would have kept an eye on her. No one needs to end up like me; bad crowd, bad friends, no way out. I'll find out who she's hanging out with and respectfully request that they cease communications with Jo Hathaway. Then I'm done. I'm losing my edge and people aren't afraid of me anymore. Gotta do something about that.

He knew how easy it was to make one small concession, then another, and then another until the problem was way beyond control. Take his life for example; a Dad who worked for the DA's office by day and became a raging alcoholic by night, a Mom who couldn't handle it anymore and vanished without a trace, and him, the kid who didn't know how to deal with all the changes and had no one to talk to. He made one tiny rebellion that led to a bigger one and then a bigger one until he had ended up the town bully and punk. He didn't want that for Jo. He didn't want that for Julie. He would do whatever he could to prevent it without them knowing and then he was done. He couldn't afford to get sidetracked now when he was so close to getting out of this town, this life.

He worked hard in school so he could get the grades he needed for admittance to the schools on the coast. Of course, having a high-profile father who just wanted to keep his deadbeat son off the radar helped. The school board decided it was best to avoid confrontations with Bruce, and especially Bruce's father, and approved his unusual request for turning in his assignments. Let his father think he was a worthless bum, it was better than having him constantly pressure him to excel. Just a little while longer and Bruce would be free. Free to walk away from this life and never look back.

But since he knew this life personally he knew it was no place for a Hathaway.

She's just a kid. I remember when I was her age. Tom was still alive, my first and best friend. I remember how I felt when they told us he was gone. That pain. That unending torture. I don't want Julie to feel that, not at all. I have to stop Jo from ruining her life somehow.

Bruce finally nodded off to a fitful sleep around four in the morning.

7

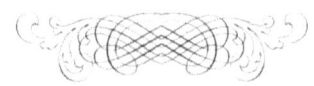

ruce decided today would be a great day to skip class, just to keep up appearances of course, and see what he could do about finding these new friends of Jo's.

It was early Monday morning and the house was a mess, as usual. Bruce checked to make sure his father was awake so he wouldn't be late for work, and then went to the kitchen to grab the cleaning supplies. He poured hot water and solvent into a basin and took the scrub brush from inside the cabinet door under the sink. He went to the first spot on the carpet and set down the basin and brush, releasing a small sigh. He wasn't sure what the stain was but he supposed his father had trouble keeping his stomach last night. There were two other stains on the living room floor but not as bad as this one. He sighed again and got to work.

Just as he was finishing the last one his father came down the stairs and stopped just inside the entryway.

"Yes, well, thank you," he harrumphed and tried again. "It's–uh–just that, well, things are so hard with your mother gone and–"

"Save it, Dad," Bruce said as he rose from the last spot and went towards the kitchen. He refused to look in his father's direction. "I don't need or want an on-again off-again father." He turned his back to him and pretended that cleaning out the supplies was of the utmost importance.

He heard his father sigh and then shuffle off to the side door. A few moments later Bruce heard the car start and his father drove away. He went out to the backyard for some fresh air; apparently the fumes were burning his eyes. Yeah, that must be it.

He lost track of time as he sat there staring at the remnants of his former life. When he rose and went back inside to resume his cleaning he noticed it was after ten. He finished repairing the damage to the house and made a sandwich for lunch while he tried to determine the best way to solve his Hathaway problem.

I guess the best place to start would be the old-style arcade and mini golf center. Jo seems to always go there and if they are who I think they are then they won't be in school either. How did she even meet up with them anyway? Talk about moving in different circles; those guys don't even go to the rich part of town at night!

He put his dish in the dishwasher and double-checked his bedroom door to make sure it was locked. Then he got on his bike and drove to the arcade.

When he got there he noticed Jake's car in the lot and planned on using his friend's presence to hide his true intentions.

"Hey Jake!" He called as he took a seat across from him at the arcade's eating area.

"Hey yourself. Why are you here? I never see you come in here," Jake replied and stuffed a slice of extremely spicy pizza in his mouth. Bruce never understood his friend's fascination with adding insane amounts of hot peppers to everything he ate. "Want a slice?"

Bruce stared down at the four remaining slices, all covered in red pepper flakes, and lost his appetite. "Nah, thanks, enjoy," he responded and waved away the server

81

instead. "I saw your car in the lot and decided to come see what you find so great about this place." Bruce said in response to Jake's earlier question.

He looked around and spotted the group of young boys and girls around age fourteen that he suspected Jo had started hanging out with over by the skeeball machines. He adjusted his position so he could watch them without appearing to and silently thanked Jake for sitting with his back to the rest of the facility. This allowed Bruce his favorite position, with his back against the wall. Bruce hated being snuck up on and preferred to keep everyone in plain sight at all times, not that he usually had much say in the matter.

Jake had asked another question and Bruce brought his wandering thoughts back to their conversation.

"Sorry, what?" he asked.

"I asked what you're really doing here. I've known you long enough to know when you're up to something, kiddo. Spill it."

"Fine, see those kids over by the skeeball machines? What do you know about them? I've seen them around town recently, but they don't look familiar to me otherwise."

Their friendship over the years meant that Jake knew when to appear uninterested and he demonstrated his ability to spy without seeming to now. A casual glance at the table behind him to search for more pepper allowed him to see the group and take in the surrounding area all at once.

"Yeah, I know 'em." Jake stared at Bruce who took the hint and nodded.

"Go ahead, I'm good for it." He responded. They may be friends, but Bruce understood it was business now.

Satisfied that Bruce knew the information he was about to reveal wasn't free Jake proceeded to tell what he knew.

"They belong to MacPherson's gang," he said quietly, "You know, the group that took over the old warehouse downtown and holds just about every business down there in the palms of their greedy little hands? Well, they recently 'acquired' some property in this part of town, this place and a few others, and they hire the dropouts and runaways to recruit for them. Promise them a place to stay and food to eat in exchange for their cooperation."

Jake glanced around and at the floor-to-ceiling mirror behind Bruce to make sure the conversation was just between the two of them. Satisfied, he continued, voice still low.

"Anyway, the younger ones, I'd say they're around

13, come here to scout. I've been watching them for a while myself. They tend to buddy up to young girls mostly, but I've seen them make nice with boys, too. Why do you want to know?"

"Just curious. Aren't they the ones that came here from Chicago? Seems to me I remember hearing about them somewhere... Yeah, they were suspected of orchestrating that politician's murder a while back, right? They couldn't trace anything back to them though, from what I remember."

"Yeah, that's them. Real smooth operators those guys. Cops can't pin a *thing* on them. They go from place to place and set up their little shops. Then when things get too hot they move on, but they always leave a group behind to manage things. The bigwigs pulled out about a month ago, but they're still here if you catch my drift. Near as I can figure they show up from time to time to check on things, rough up some of their boys, take their share of the money and so on then leave again for greener pastures." Jake said and downed another slice of pizza.

"Great, so they could be back anytime..." Bruce trailed off. He began to wonder just how deep Jo Hathaway was with this gang. Did she know who they really were? She couldn't or she would have nothing to do with them. He was sure of that; as sure as he was that he was getting out of this place as soon as possible. He wanted to know if Jake had seen her there; that would tell him more than anything else if Jo was in serious trouble. If she was, how could he tell Julie? Bruce tuned back in since Jake was still talking.

"...and so that's why I think they won't be around until next month. Hey, are you listening?"

"Yeah, so let me ask you something. Have you seen them talking to a young girl about eleven?" and he gave Jake the description of the girl he remembered from a little while ago. He didn't realize it at the time, but Jo reminded him very much of a young Julie. The girl he fell for before his world fell apart. Julie's hair had gotten darker over time, but Jo was the spitting image of her older sister at the same age.

"Yeah, she's in here a lot. She giggles when the boys pay attention to her and whispers in the girls' ears. She has no idea what they're about. Why? You know her?"

Bruce met his eyes and waited.

"Right. So anyway, I think they've chosen that girl for whatever it is they chose people for. I don't think it's anything good. If you know her you should warn her." Jake said and finished off the pizza. "You really should have tried a slice; it was something special. Got it just right this time."

Bruce just smiled and got up from the table. As he walked passed he slipped a fifty on the table next to Jake's plate.

"Not a chance, bro. I don't want an inferno in my mouth. See ya 'round."

Bruce drove around for a long time contemplating what he should do and how to tell Julie. He drove downtown to the old warehouse district and looked around, pretending to be lost. He saw the place Jake mentioned and didn't like the looks of it. He knew the police had their hands full with all the crime that took place in that district and it wasn't any wonder that this place was here. The windows were boarded, the stairs leading to the back office were weak and rotting and several were missing, the driveway was in dire need of repaving, and there were two domineering men guarding the entrance. Interesting.

Why post a guard for a rundown old warehouse unless you were hiding something? I'd better go before I draw attention to myself.

He looked at his watch and realized he was going to be late for meeting Julie. He pulled out his phone from the compartment on the back of his bike and appeared to realize he was in the wrong place. He threw up his hands, pretending to be frustrated and drove directly for the nearest main road. He drove in circles for a bit in case he was being followed, and then took the street that led to the youth center.

On the way he tried to rehearse what he would tell Julie. He was really worried about her sister now. He had thought she was hanging out with a bad crowd, but he had no idea just how bad they really were. He was glad he ran into Jake! His old friend always knew about the goings on around town; who was who, what they did, how to find them. He wondered why Jake never finished college; he had been a junior now for three years. Usually Jake just acquired information, but when he thought something bad was about to happen or someone was in danger he always left an anonymous tip at the police station. Jake may be a loser, but he had his merits.

And he certainly came in handy today! He must be worried about that gang to have gone to so much trouble to find out about them. Jo has no idea what she's getting into. What if they take her somewhere? Trafficking has gotten to be a huge problem and she's just the kind someone would take and sell to the highest bidder. She must have her doubts, suspicions. She has to know they aren't good people to be around. She couldn't be that

87

blind, could she? How do I tell Julie? She'll be devastated...

Just then Bruce turned the final corner before coming to the youth center and heard a scream.

8

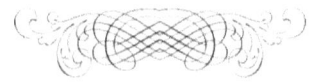

Julie had trouble focusing all day. She couldn't remember a single thing she learned in school that day or who she spoke to in passing. Her thoughts were consumed with her sister and how she failed her. No matter how hard Julie tried she just seemed to keep making a mess of things. Now she was struggling to help the last few students at the youth center. Poor Chloe had to ask her three times to look over her math homework before Julie realized she was needed.

I've got to focus. The kids need me and in just two weeks the center will be gone. They just can't stay open without funding and our biggest donator pulled out. What will they do then? What will I do then? I love working here...

She tried her best to pay attention to little Chloe, the seven year old that was struggling with math, but she simply could not concentrate for more than a few minutes. Finally, she asked Jessica, one of the other workers, to assist Chloe while she took a few minutes break.

She sat in the back room of the center by the offices and nursed a bottle of water. She reviewed her last conversation with her sister, but that only made her want to cry. She had let Jo down in the worst possible way and she had no idea how to make it right. Instead, she decided to focus on Bruce and how much he had softened towards her lately.

Who would have ever thought that I would become friends with Bruce again? He used to be so unmerciful towards me since we were freshman. I recall that he went away just after his brother died for about six months or so, then he came back different, changed. He was mean and bullied just about everyone. He was so incredibly angry and no one could reach him. He just shut everyone out, everyone, even those of us that were his friends before he left. Now... well he's mellowed at any rate but he's still a tough guy.

Julie paused in her reflections to wonder if she was somehow responsible for his change. She remembered praying that he would find a friend; although she was sure she also mentioned that she didn't want that friend to be her! *Suppose... just suppose God sent him to me... what if I really* am *that friend? No, that couldn't be right. It was just coincidence that he wasn't mean to me anymore. Just coincidence. Nothing more. Right?* Julie didn't believe in coincidence.

With a sigh Julie rose from her perch and threw her empty water bottle in the recycle bin. There was still an hour left until the youth center closed and a few more students had wandered in while she was gone.

She approached a boy of about ten who looked like he needed help with his science project. After about half an hour they were able to complete his project and his mother returned to pick him up. He was the last child in the center so the manager let everyone who wanted to leave early clock out. Julie decided to stay in order to help clean up and prepare the facility for the next day. Unfortunately, with no students to help, her mind wandered back to her sister.

Jo was being sent away at the end of the semester in just five more weeks. Would they let her stay for

Christmas? Surely they must! Because of her distraction she was not paying attention to her surroundings when she left the center.

It's all my fault somehow, though I admit I still can't see where I failed her. I wish I had paid more attention to her! I could have warned her sooner or spent time with her so she wouldn't need to seek friends elsewhere. Now she's angry with me for trying to talk to her! How can I –

At that moment she heard the sound of footsteps behind her. She turned just as a man wearing a ski mask came within grasping range. As she realized her situation was dire she tried to run. She had just enough time to scream before her attacker grabbed her. He wrapped one arm around her throat and used the other to pin her arms to her side. Then a second attacker appeared to her right, where she had her purse hanging at her side. He started to reach for it when he suddenly lurched forward as if struck from behind. As he stumbled forward a figure appeared in Julie's vision and she breathed a sigh of relief. There was Bruce!

The sudden appearance of another person distracted the first attacker and bought Julie the time she needed to free her arms. It only took a split second, but that was all she needed.

She bent at the waist and side-stepped to the man's

92

choking arm. She rained blows to his midsection with her inside arm and as he tried to protect himself she grabbed his choke arm and snapped it over her shoulder, effectively breaking his arm. He cried out in pain yet still tried to grab her.

She sent a swift kick to his midsection and delivered a hammer blow to the back of his head as he fell to his knees, knocking him unconscious. She glanced over to Bruce and noticed that he was still holding his own against the second attacker.

Bruce and the second attacker were grappling and exchanging blows not far from Julie and her attacker. Bruce got the upper hand and swung his elbow into the man's face. As he spun around Bruce grabbed him in a Full Nelson, kicked his knees so that he would fall to the ground. Bruce knew he needed to end this fight quickly, so he knocked the assailant unconscious in a few quick moves. The entire fight was over in seconds.

Bruce ran over to Julie and held her shaking form close.

"I—I—thank you," she managed to stutter out before she broke down.

Bruce stroked her hair and made comforting sounds as he gently rocked her from side to side. The manager of the youth center came out and hurried over to them.

"She's alright, just shaken up. Call the police and tell them to come pick these guys up. I'll see she gets home alright after they take her statement." Bruce guided Julie over to the building and they waited inside until the police came.

Julie was still so shaken after the officer got their statements that she had trouble finding her keys so she could drive home.

"Nothing doin', Hathaway." Bruce covered her nervous hands with his own large one. "I'll take you home. You're in no condition to drive right now anyway. If you don't mind riding on the bike, that is. I've got an extra helmet that should fit you."

Julie just nodded and let him lead the way. He wrapped an arm around her and she felt such strength and safety there that she started crying all over again.

"I'm sorry, I don't know why I'm crying, it's just—"

"Shh, hush now. You have every reason to be upset, Julie. You were just assaulted and almost mugged. Go ahead and let it out. I'll wait."

She turned into his shoulder and released all her anxiety over the past several weeks, her fears for her sister, her resolve to protect Jo from harm, her fright at the attack tonight, her guilt over not paying closer attention to her surroundings, her worry that her

94

distractions had caused Bruce harm—

"Are you hurt?" she gasped when she suddenly realized she hadn't made sure *he* was alright. She started to check for injuries when he just laughed and smiled down at her.

"Nothing I haven't been through before. Don't you worry. Come on, let's get you home."

He helped her with the helmet and goggles, and gave her a few instructions for riding on a motorcycle.

"First, I've carried lots of passengers on this bike and I know how it handles. I will keep you safe. Have you ever ridden on one of these?" Bruce asked. When Julie shook her head he continued coaching her on what to expect.

"Ok, keep your hands around my waist, and stay away from this part here," he pointed to the engine and exhaust. "It gets hot, real hot! Keep your feet here on the footrests and remember to lean into the turns. Don't fight them! It will unbalance us and we may spin off. Follow my lead. You can talk to me through the helmet, it's linked to mine. And last, put on this extra jacket. You'll need it. If you can do all of that, I will handle the rest. Deal?" When he was sure she understood he did one final safety check of her and the bike and then they started off.

Julie wrapped her arms tightly around his waist as she was instructed and leaned her head against his shoulder. She had never been on a motorcycle before, but she wasn't afraid. Somehow she knew Bruce would never let anything happen to her.

9

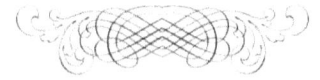

Bruce could still smell the soft scent of vanilla from her perfume and the feel of her silky hair against his skin when he rested his chin on the top of her head. She fit quite nicely there. It felt good to hold her. Too good. Try as he might, he couldn't help caring for this girl. And now she was riding on the back of his bike, arms wrapped snugly around him and head resting against his back.

So much for my image. I knew it, she got me. I knew it would happen, but I just didn't want to stop it. I've never been so scared in my life. I heard that scream, her scream, and thought I would lose her. I never want to feel that way again. Anything coulda happened. She coulda been killed. I coulda been killed. I've been trained for fights involving weapons, but I never actually had to try it before. Glad they were just petty thieves. Or were they? Could they be related to all this? Best not go there, Weber. Just get her home safe, that's all you need to do right now.

"It's a left turn up here, ain't it?" Bruce called over his shoulder as he waited for his turn at a traffic light.

"Yeah, second house on the right. How'd you know?"

"I remember from when we were kids, that's all, but it has been awhile."

"Yeah, I had the whole fifth grade class over for my birthday and you were there. I had forgotten about that. I don't even remember what I got from everyone. You probably don't even remember what you gave me, do you?"

Bruce knew exactly what he had given her. That was when he first started to like her, shyly, but even so he wanted to give her something she would remember. It was a little case for pencils or pens. But it wasn't the case itself so much as the cartoon characters on it, her favorite at the time.

"It was a pencil case with your favorite cartoon on it." Bruce replied.

"That was from you? I still have it. Sits on my desk. I

98

use it all the time, actually. It was the perfect gift. I'm sorry I didn't remember it was from you." Julie said and laid her head against his back again.

"No worries, I'm glad you got some use out of it," he said as the light changed.

He pulled into her driveway and helped her off.

"Listen," he said, "I have something I need to talk to you and your parents about. Mind if I come in?"

"No, not at all," she replied.

Her parents met them at the door, alarmed by the sound of his motor in their driveway.

"Evenin' sir, ma'am," Bruce said, "May I come inside? There's something I think you should know."

They nodded their permission and Julie led the way into the living room.

"Mom, Dad, this is my friend Bruce. He came to my rescue tonight. Don't panic, I'm fine, but I was attacked at the youth center. If it weren't for Bruce I don't know what would have happened." Julie said as she sat down on the sofa and beckoned Bruce, who was trailing after her parents, to join her. He stood awkwardly at the end of the sofa, and shuffled from one foot to the other. He was having difficulty deciding where to put his hands, in his pockets or at his side. He finally decided to sit at the end of the sofa, far away from Julie, and rested his elbows on his knees.

Meanwhile, Julie's parents were fussing over her and asking what happened. Bruce tuned back in to the conversation when they asked him how he came to be there just in time.

"I was just out—" he started.

"He usually meets—" Julie said at the same time.

They shared a nervous laugh and Bruce answered the question.

"I noticed a while back that Julie works late down there so I decided to meet her after work and make sure she was safe. Lots of things happen down there, and well, she shouldn't be walking alone down there, that's all." His fidgeting started all over again and the temperature rose at least ten degrees, he was sure.

Julie noticed his discomfort and threw him a lifeline.

"You said there was something you wanted to tell us, right Bruce?"

"Uh, yeah," he replied, relieved. "I found out some things today. Uh, *ahem*."

Now that the moment had arrived, he didn't know where to begin. *Should I tell them I skipped school? Nah, bad idea. But I don't wanna lie, either...*

Again, Julie noticed his nervousness and interceded.

"I noticed you were out sick today. Is everything

alright?"

Bruce shot her a quick thank you with his eyes and launched in to his story.

"Yeah, but around two I decided I just needed some air, so I went down to that gaming center, the one with mini golf and an old 80s style arcade. Do you know it?" When they glanced at each other and nodded in the affirmative he continued. "Well, my friend Jake was there so I sat down and talked with him. Say, is your sister here?" He turned to Julie.

Dr. Hathaway answered, "Yes, but she's upstairs studying. Does this have something to do with her?"

"Yes, sir, it does, and she won't like what I have to say. Can she hear us?"

"Not well, but we can go to the study if you like. The sound doesn't travel there." Mrs. Hathaway led the way to the study and they all sat down in the oversized leather chairs.

Bruce removed his leather jacket and took a quick look around. He saw three walls lined from ceiling to floor with books and the fourth wall housed a fireplace with a stone hearth and a flatscreen television over the mantel. The wall directly across from the entry also held a bay window with throw pillows forming a small seat. *Nice place,* he thought to himself, *so different from mine.*

We never had it so good even before...

He brought his thoughts back to the task at hand and continued his story.

"Thank you, sir, ma'am. As I was saying, my friend Jake was there so I sat and talked with him for a while. Julie had mentioned that her sister was getting into trouble a lot and I promised I would look into it for her. I had a suspicion that Johannah was mixing with a bad crowd, so I followed a hunch. There were a group of kids, guess they were around thirteen or so, some older, at the arcade. I had seen this group before, they seldom go to school and they're always together, but I didn't recognize them as from around here, you know? Riverside pretty much doesn't change. People don't move out and very few move in. So I asked Jake if he knew anything about them," he paused and silently asked if it was okay to continue. He had their undivided attention. It was almost as if they were starving for this information and he finally understood how worried they were for Johannah. *Wow, no one ever worries about me that way. 'Cept maybe Mrs. M... Must be nice. Don't screw it up, Jo...*

"Well, he knew a lot about them and that's why I'm here. Johannah's in trouble. Big trouble. Those kids belong to an 'organization' if you can call it that, the

102

MacPherson Gang. Have you heard of them? They were suspected in that politician's murder in Chicago a while back, but it was never proved. Anyway, it seems this group travels across the country and recruits dropouts and runaways. They offer them a place to stay and food to eat in exchange for running favors for them. That bunch of kids at the arcade does just that. Jake says they make friends with young girls mostly, and he had seen Johannah with them several times. He didn't know why, but he didn't think it was for anything good.

"Anyway, he told me that they now own most of the businesses in the warehouse district, so I went down there to see if I could find out anything else. Have you ever heard people say the hairs on the back of their neck stand out? Well, I never believed it before, but when I saw that warehouse I did. They had two guards posted outside a rundown empty warehouse. I hightailed it out of there and that's when I went to meet Julie. You know the rest." He sat back and relaxed now that the hard part was over.

The room was so quiet that he could hear the hum of the refrigerator in the kitchen down the hall. He figured they needed to digest what he just told them and realized it probably didn't make them feel any better.

"Sorry to spring all that on you, but if she really is

mixed up with them I thought you should know," he stood up to leave. "I'll be going now."

Mrs. Hathaway shook her head as if to clear it and stood up. "I'm sorry, Bruce, it's just so much to take in. Thank you very much for everything you've done for our girls. We are deeply indebted to you. That was a very dangerous thing you did by going down to that warehouse, and I am so very grateful—" she broke down in tears and could not continue.

Dr. Hathaway went over to her and wrapped an arm around her shoulders.

"Yes, thank you very much, son," he said, "You risked your life twice today for us. There must be some way we can repay your kindness. Will you allow us to see you home? Or maybe you would like to come over for dinner one night? It seems so inadequate, but..."

"Ah, no, thank you, sir," Bruce began shuffling from one foot to the other as he stood by the door. "Really, it's no problem. Guys like me, well, we can go places others can't and no one pays us any attention. I should really get going. Glad I was there to help."

He wasn't sure if it would be appropriate to just turn and leave, but he really wanted to be anywhere else at that moment. He was sure the temperature in that room was warmer than it was in the living room, and he fidgeted with the leather jacket he was holding.

Julie stood and offered to walk him out. He could have kissed her right then and there, but decided against it. She seemed to have developed an uncanny ability to read his mind lately.

As they stepped outside and approached his motorcycle she reached out and touched his arm. He stopped midstride and turned to her.

"Thank you, Bruce, for saving me and possibly for saving my sister. You have no idea how much that means to me. It's funny, if anyone had told me back in September that we would be here like this I would have laughed them right out of Riverside, but... here we are. Friends. At least, I hope we're friends." Julie tilted her head to the side and looked up at him. A slight smile curved at the corners of her mouth.

Mesmerized by the sincerity in her grey eyes all he could do was nod. Inwardly shaking himself he said, "Sure, Hathaway, anything you say." He gave her a cocky smile and put on his helmet so she couldn't see how much her words affected him.

"I'm not fooled for a second, Weber!" Julie stepped back as he started the engine and backed out of the driveway.

"You're infuriating!" He called.

"Thank you!" She called back.

He risked one more glance at her from the street and waved good-bye. *Shouldn't've done that, Weber. Look at her standing there in the moonlight. The breeze in her hair. Ack, you got it bad. Listen to you waxing poetic. Go home, Weber, go home.*

He pulled away without another glance and drove home. When he got there, though, his night was far from over.

Distracted by his last glimpse of Julie and the events of the evening he forgot to shut off the motor at the corner and wheel it home. He didn't realize his mistake until he reached for the front door. He could hear his father destroying the house again and cursing at his worthless son.

"Get in this house, Boy," he bellowed and Bruce had no choice but to obey. He hoped the neighbors didn't hear, wouldn't hear, but there was little chance of that. The houses were too close together.

Bruce gathered his strength and opened the door.

10

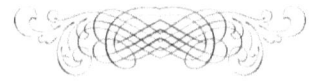

Bruce decided today would be another great day to be out sick again. Not for appearances, but for *his* appearance. His father roughed him up pretty bad this time and he didn't want anyone seeing him. For the life of him he didn't understand why things had to be this way. Sure, things were hard after Tom died, but did they have to end up like this? Did his mom have to leave? Did Dad have to drink so much? Couldn't they have found some way to work things out so that he didn't feel abandoned and unwanted? After seeing how much Julie's parents loved their children he felt even more alone. *Do they realize what a good thing they have?* He wondered as he grabbed another ice pack from the freezer for his eye.

It was about two in the afternoon and he had finally been able to move around without aggravating his bruised ribs from when he recoiled and fell over an end table. Even wearing a shirt hurt and the fabric was even now rubbing against the scratches on his arms and chest. He set down the ice pack and looked around at the mayhem caused by their fight last night. He managed to evade most of the tirade, but he still caught some of his father's anger. He refused to hit back, though. He wouldn't disrespect the memory of his family like his father did. He bent over to pick up the corner table that had somehow been knocked over, but the strain on his ribs was too much. Instead he lifted it with his foot to a height he could grab and then set it to rights.

The rest will have to wait. I can't clean it all up right now, but I'd better have it done by the time he gets home. No way I'm staying here tonight.

He went into the kitchen to fix a bacon and tomato sandwich for his lunch and noticed the stack of dirty dishes for the first time. *What did he do, use every dish we have? I just did these yesterday.* He loaded them into the dishwasher and started it, but instead of preparing his lunch he just sat at the table and laid his head gingerly in his hands.

He was hurt and he was angry but most of all he was sad. He had never felt so lost in his entire life. He wasn't even sure why he tried so hard to please his father anymore. He blamed himself for his father's behavior and that's what truly caused the change in Bruce, but it wasn't long before he just came to resent the man. Still, he thought that if he could just keep him quiet by doing the things his mother used to do his dad would leave him alone. Unfortunately he could never do them well enough. No matter what he did it was wrong; no matter what he said it was wrong. Eventually he came to the realization that there was simply no way to make his father happy. No matter how hard he tried. Tom made him happy. Bruce made him angry. That was all there was to it. *Why? Why do things have to be this way? Why can't he just accept me? I'm not Tom but I still have worth, don't I? Maybe I don't. Maybe I really am irredeemable like he says. I have to get out of here, run away, something. I can't take it anymore!*

The clock chimed the top of the next hour and he rose from the table to make his sandwich. He carried the weight of the world on his shoulders and his steps dragged from the burden. Just as he was finishing up the doorbell rang.

Strange, who could that be? No one ever visits us.

He waded through the broken glass, papers, and other debris resulting from the altercation and his father's drunken stumbling and opened the door.

"Hi Br— oh!" Julie gasped once she saw the black and blue pulp that was Bruce's face at the moment. "Oh no! What happened? Are you alright?"

Bruce was so surprised to see her that he did nothing to prevent her from entering the house. Too late he realized his error. He should have left the door unanswered. He should have pretended he wasn't home. He should have... he should have...*done something!*

"What are you doing here? How did you even find me? You have to leave, now!" He grabbed her arm and tried to maneuver her to the door again, but she wrenched away and stood in the middle of the destruction.

"You're in the school directory, remember? The same way you found *my* number? Bruce, what happened here? The place is a mess and," she paused and noticed the grimace Bruce was trying to hide.

When Julie pulled away from him she accidentally bumped his bruised ribs. It was all he could do to fight the urge to cry out in agony. He couldn't prevent his

110

hand from going to his side, however and that's what Julie latched on to.

"What's wrong? Why are you holding your side like that?" She came to him and lifted the edge of his shirt. Another gasp escaped her lips and her hands covered her mouth. "Oh Bruce! We have to get you to a hospital; your ribs could be broken!" The worry was etched plainly on her face and it melted Bruce's heart.

"No! No doctor's. I'm fine; I just have to take it easy for a while. Please go, there's nothing you can do here. Wild party last night, that's all. Now you have to go, please."

How could he have been so stupid? How could he have let her see this? See him? He worked so hard at hiding this part of his life and now... now...

"No way, at least put some ice on it. The kitchen is through here, right? This house is laid out like a friend of mine's. You go sit down and I'll be right back."

Bruce could do nothing to stop her. Every move sent waves of sheer agony throughout his body. She must have hit him harder than he thought. Or maybe they *were* broken? Nah, it would be worse than this if they were really broken. Julie returned momentarily with the ice pack he had discarded earlier. She carefully placed it against his side and brushed back the hair that had fallen

111

over his forehead.

"Tell me what happened, Bruce, please," she asked, a crease formed on her brow and she appeared to be fighting back tears.

"Nothing. I told you, wild party. You know me, always getting into trouble." It was a weak attempt and he knew it the moment he said it.

"Can't fool me, Weber, remember?" she said as she continued to stroke his hair.

It felt so nice to be cared for. Bruce couldn't remember a time when anyone showed this much concern for him. And the fact that it was Julie made it hurt that much more. He leaned into her embrace and rested his head on her shoulder. It felt so good to just rest... just for a moment...

Abruptly, too abruptly in fact, he stood and pulled her off the sofa. Rather harshly he ushered her to the door.

"You can't understand. No one does. Just leave, Hathaway. I don't want you here, and I won't risk losing you this way!" He held open the door and waited for her to leave.

"I'll go, but this isn't over. Don't think for a second that I'm gonna let this go. Something is very wrong here and I wouldn't be any kind of friend if I let it continue. I *am* your friend, Bruce. You can trust me. I trust you. You saved my life, now let me save yours. You know where to find me if you want to talk." She turned to leave and hesitated on the steps. "I'll pray for you, Bruce. I'll pray that you learn to trust and find help."

Bruce saw the tears fall then. But not just from Julie, his tears were falling, too. He silently closed the door.

Bruce went back to the kitchen and sat at the table. He made no effort to stop the tears; he needed them, this time, because he realized that he could no longer see Julie. At all. Ever. He thought it would be alright to pursue her, even if only as a friend, but now he fully understood the weight of that decision. No one can ever know what his life was like. They wouldn't understand that it was *his* fault things were this way. He made bad choices in recent years and this was the consequence. He would pay his penance. Save him? No, he didn't deserve saving.

Now more than ever Bruce realized the magnitude of the way things were and what that meant for him. Maybe someday he would come back and see her, if she was still here. He would congratulate her on her marriage and praise her beautiful children, but he was as far removed from her world as the serpent was from the dove. There could never be a way for him to be worthy of her, not anymore. He pretended that things would be fine as long as no one knew the truth, but he couldn't hide it any longer. He was sure Julie would tell her parents or her best friends. Then people would come around investigating, poking their noses into his family business. That would make his father really angry. It would be in the news and the whole town would start whispering behind his back.

No! I have to make sure no one finds out. Not yet, not until I'm ready to leave. Then I don't care what happens. But for now no one can find out. I have to make her understand that. Somehow...

Bruce strengthened his resolve to keep people out of his life. No matter the cost, he was in this alone. He had to be. He knew the full extent of his father's wrath and if people started poking around there would be no end to his fury. Julie could get hurt, bad. He would rather saw off his leg than have her go through even a fraction of what he endured every day. She was too pure and innocent for that. No one deserved that. Well, no one but him. He more than deserved it and he would face it alone. All alone. And that was a promise.

Bruce didn't want anyone asking him questions the

next day at school so he played up the tough guy routine full force. He was angry now, very angry, and he didn't care who knew it. He knocked into someone once and just glared at the poor kid until she apologized. He took her books anyway and threw them in the trashcan down the hallway. He turned another corner and ran headlong into Julie.

"Oh! Bruce! I'm sorry, I didn't see you there. Are you alright, how are your ribs?"

Bruce figured now was as good a time as any to set her straight, so he took her arm and led her down the hallway to an empty classroom.

"Listen Hathaway, whatever you think you know you're wrong. And whatever you think is happening between us you're wrong. Stay out of my life and out of my way, got it?" Bruce towered over her for emphasis and poured all the animosity he could into his face.

"But it doesn't reach your eyes, Bruce," she said softly. "You can't hide the truth because your eyes always give you away, did you know that?"

Taken aback, Bruce stepped away from her. "What are you talking about, Hathaway? I meant what I said, stay out of it!"

"No, I can't do that Bruce. Your father hits you. He has no right! It has to stop, Bruce. No one deserves that,

115

ever!"

"What do you know about it!? Do you even know *anything* about me!?" Bruce bellowed. A student passing by peeked into the classroom and Bruce realized he was talking too loud. He went over to the door and slammed it in the student's face.

"Don't yell at me, Bruce! I'm trying to help you!"

"Well, I don't need your help, Hathaway. Leave me alone! Got it, stay out!"

"No! I won't! I know you're angry and you think something terrible will happen if anyone learns about your father, but he needs to be stopped. You have to talk to someone, anyone. You have to get out of there, Bruce, before he kills you!"

"I can handle it. Besides, I'll be gone soon enough and I'm *never* coming back."

"Bruce..." Julie pleaded with him to understand.

"If you thought I was bad before, just wait. If you so much as hint about this to anyone—"

"Fine! I won't say anything, *this time*. But if I see you hurt again I will and I don't care how many empty threats you make. I care about you and I won't let him hurt you anymore!" Julie stormed out of the classroom and down the hall before Bruce could respond. He punched the wall and went to his next class.

116

11

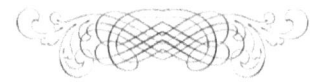

Julie stormed down the hallway towards her next class. Neal caught up with her and asked if she was alright.

"Just a friend in trouble, that's all. I'm just anxious and upset, Neal. Sorry to worry you."

"Yeah, I saw you talking to Bruce. What's going on?"

"I can't tell you right now, I made a promise. Just pray for him, Neal, and get everyone you can think of to pray, too. He needs it. That's all I can say."

"Sure, but can you at least tell me if he's put you in any danger?"

"No, he hasn't. He wouldn't, but *his* life is in danger, Neal! I'm so frightened for him!" Julie could do nothing to stop the waver in her voice or the tears from pooling in her eyes. "Please don't ask me anymore questions, just pray." She left him wondering and went into her next class.

She struggled through her remaining classes and was relieved when the final bell rang. She drove home in a fog and could only assume the Lord was steering her vehicle because she couldn't remember ever getting in the car. She didn't even check the machine for messages or see if her mother left her a note. Instead, she went to her room and closed the door. She had a lot of thinking to do.

Why did I make that promise? He needs help! And here I am thinking my problems are the worst problems anyone could ever have. Talk about a reality check! I've been so petty and foolish. Here my friend has been suffering unimaginably for years and I did nothing! I even tried to avoid him! How incredibly selfish!

She set her things down by the desk and curled up on her bed. She couldn't begin to understand how much Bruce had suffered over the years, but she knew he was in pain. Now that she thought about it, his behavior over the past few years had to be his way of crying out for help. Did anyone know? Did anyone realize what was happening to him?

Maybe not, she thought, *he has gotten pretty adept at shutting people out. Maybe no one knows... How awful! To have to face that all alone! Well, he isn't alone anymore, he has me, whether he likes it or not!*

She turned over and saw her Bible sitting on the nightstand. She reached for it and let the book fall open on its own. Sometimes she would let the Lord guide her to the passage He wanted her to read and she felt that gentle nudging now. The book opened to the 43rd chapter of Isaiah. She read verses one through four: "...Fear not, for I have redeemed you; I have called you by name, you are mine. When you pass through the waters, I will be with you; when you walk through fire you shall not be burned, and the flame shall not consume you...Because you are precious in my eyes, and honored, and I love you..."

What is it, Lord? What are You trying to tell me? Or is this for Bruce? Should I give him this verse? Does he need the hope these words contain? Does he feel that he somehow deserves what's happening to him? That just isn't true! Lord, help me help him. Open his heart to this message and whisper to him. Show him where to go and guide his steps. Give me the words to say that will help him

119

or lead me to someone who can. Only You know what is really going on there, Lord. I pray You hold him in Your arms and protect him from harm. I think You know how much he means to me, but let Your will be done, not mine. Amen.

She felt a peace wash over her and she knew that somehow she needed to get these verses to Bruce. The pieces were falling into place and her eyes were opened to his plight. She was certain that he blamed himself – that he felt irredeemable – but she had yet to figure out for what and why.

She mulled over the past several years since Tom Weber died. She was young then, only twelve, and Bruce went by Michael. It was announced to the students the day after it happened. She wanted to go visit him and talk to him, be a friend, but she was scared she would say the wrong thing. She never went and Michael never came back. He missed the rest of that semester and the next year; their last year in junior high. There were rumors that he was sent off to some special school for kids going through tragedy, but she had never heard of such a place and doubted the stories.

When they started their freshman year of high school he came back, but he was different. He was incredibly mean and bullied everyone. He refused to answer to his given name and instead used his middle name, Bruce. Julie avoided him like the plague. She didn't like what he had become, but she saw no reason to question it. People changed; it happened all the time, especially in high school.

Back then he used to pick on her incessantly. He would put gum in her hair or throw her books in the trash. Once he went through her purse when she stepped out for a minute and when she came back all of her things were glued to her desk. She thought she would die of mortification. He just laughed; laughed as she started to cry. The teacher did nothing. Well, that wasn't entirely true. Bruce did get detention, but Julie always wondered why no one stopped him.

When they were sophomores he mellowed a bit but still made life miserable for her. He started skipping class a lot back then and getting into fights. Was that when the hitting started? Julie contemplated the timing of that year. Bruce learned how to drive earlier than the rest of the class, but he was also one of the oldest ones in their class. About six months older than Julie, she recalled. He somehow ended up with a motorcycle and Julie questioned the wisdom in that decision since that was what Tom was driving when he died. That was also about the time Julie stopped noticing his mother around town. They used to always run into each other when Mrs. Hathaway went grocery shopping. The two mothers weren't friends, but they were always cordial to each other.

If Bruce's mom left or was badly hurt then that would explain a great deal. He would have lost his brother and his mother in a short span of time. Maybe his father, too, if Mr. Weber was being abusive at that time.

Poor Bruce! Julie thought to herself. *I had no idea things were that bad! That must be what happened; they never got over losing Tom. They never found a way to deal with life without him and they all fell apart. How sad! Someone should have been able to do something to prevent it; someone had to notice. Or did they all turn a blind eye like I did...?*

That thought brought her up short. Julie had always prided herself on being there for everyone, helping them solve their problems, and being a support when they needed it. Now she realized she wasn't there for the one person who needed it most in her life. Perhaps that was why Bruce picked on her so much. Maybe he saw someone who could help him, but he didn't understand it all himself. Maybe he was lost and confused and his parents weren't there for him so he misbehaved in an attempt to get *someone* to pay attention to him. But it didn't work. Everyone just wrote him off as a problem child and avoided him.

Julie began to wonder if God was giving her this glimpse into Bruce's life so that she could understand how He felt when He watched Bruce, His lost child. Julie grieved in a way she never had before. She grieved for Bruce, for Tom, for Mr. and Mrs. Weber, for the time lost, and the tragic end to what was once a happy family. She lay on her bed for hours and cried and prayed for her friend.

When she had drained all her tears and emptied her heart to the Lord she roused and went to the top of the stairs. She stopped before descending because she could overhear quite an argument going on downstairs. She was so wrapped up in her thoughts she didn't even notice Jo and her parents had come home. She didn't mean to eavesdrop, but the discussion was heated and she wanted to be on hand if she was needed.

Jo was fighting vehemently with her parents about going to Sioux Falls. They wanted to enroll her in a Christian girls' school close to where their grandparents lived for one year. If Jo demonstrated she could be trusted they would let her come home. Jo insisted they were being unreasonable and if they would just listen to her they would see that she wasn't doing anything wrong. Dr. Hathaway questioned her choice of friends lately and that just set Jo off again. To Julie it sounded like both sides were tired and angry and neither was listening to the other anymore. She came downstairs to try to cool things off for a bit, but Jo used the distraction to run upstairs and slam her bedroom door.

"I'm sorry. I thought if I interrupted things would cool down a bit. I didn't think she would leave."

"It's not your fault, Julie," her dad said, "We weren't getting anywhere anyway. I really do think it's for the best that she goes to your grandparents after Christmas. We have to get her away from those new friends, if that's what they are."

"I agree, but is sending her away the best answer? I just feel like we're dumping our problems on Gramma and Grandpa. Won't she just resent us all the more? I don't know, I just think it would make things worse, not better."

"I don't know either, but sometimes tough love is the answer," Mrs. Hathaway replied. "We can't continue to do nothing and she will not listen to reason. I see no other alternative."

"But this isn't your problem, Julie. Let us handle it. Have you eaten dinner yet?" Her father asked.

"No, I came down to see if I could fix anything, but I

124

didn't realize you were all home already. I've been thinking about Bruce and how I can be a friend to him. I'm no closer to an answer to that question then you are about Jo."

"Well, I'm sure you'll figure it out. You have a discerning heart and you always think things through." Her mother sat down in a nearby chair and rubbed her temples. "We haven't started anything; do you want to order out instead? I'm not very hungry right now, but you can get something for you and your sister."

"I have to go soon, so don't order anything for me, sweetheart," Dr. Hathaway called to Julie as he entered the study.

"Alright," she replied. She went to find her sister and ask if she wanted anything.

"Jo?" She knocked on the door. "It's just me. Are you hungry? I could order out."

"No," came her sister's reply. "Just leave me alone!"

Julie sighed and went downstairs again. She told her mother she was just going to eat a snack since no one wanted dinner and asked if she would like some tea.

"No, dear, but thank you. I think I'll go lie down for a while. Will you wake me in an hour? I have an important meeting tomorrow and I want to go over my notes again."

Julie assured her mom that she would wake her on time and rummaged in the pantry for a snack. She pulled out the bread and decided to make a bacon and tomato sandwich. After fixing her meager meal she sat down in the breakfast room and worried about the problems in her own family. She didn't think they were falling apart, but she was concerned that things were changing. Until recently things had always been great. The siblings got along; they seldom fought with each other. Her parents still looked at each other like newlyweds. They were never without food or shelter. They weren't rich, but they were well off. She struggled to imagine the pain of losing any one of them. She couldn't do it. She just did not want to think of life without Josh or Jo, Mom or Dad. She had no idea how anyone could endure it. She knew the pain she felt knowing that her sister was leaving, but it paled in comparison to what Bruce must have felt when his brother died. A pain that never ceased for him. A raw, gaping, bleeding hole in his heart that he believed nothing could fill.

Julie gained a new perspective on life after witnessing the turmoil in Bruce's. It was like she was seeing for miles instead of only a few feet. It freed her in ways she never thought possible, but also burdened her with the enormity of sorrow both in the world and right in her own backyard.

But she couldn't think about that right now. One thing at a time, and now it was time to rouse her mother, so she cleaned up the remains of her dinner and went upstairs.

12

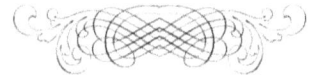

*A*fter school on Thursday, Julie decided to visit the school library in search of information on child abuse and domestic violence. As she was perusing the school's limited selection of books and resources Mrs. Mayweather approached her.

"I noticed you were not having much luck, my dear. Is there anything I can help you find?" Mrs. Mayweather asked.

"Well, I'm looking for books about domestic violence. A friend of mine may be in trouble, but I don't know how to help him. I was hoping something here would provide some guidance."

"My! That's a heavy topic! We don't have very much here on that, but the public library has a much better selection. You could also go online and search the county's Public Health and Human Services page. Or I could direct you to some national organizations. If you truly believe your friend is in trouble, though, you are obligated to tell the authorities, my dear. It is the law in every state in the country, after all."

"I know, but I don't want to do that until I'm sure. I only suspect and what if I'm wrong? I could ruin what's left of his family. I need to know more…" Julie trailed off as she stared at the shelves in front of her.

There were several books on child abuse in manufacturing plants several decades ago, but nothing recent. She knew from her history courses that those very cases were what caused the government to create the child labor laws still in effect. It was a fascinating topic to her, but not what she needed right now.

"May I ask who it is?" Mrs. Mayweather was still talking to her, but Julie wasn't paying attention.

"I'm sorry," she said, "What did you just ask me?"

"I asked, who is your friend? I have a friend in trouble, too, and I hope it isn't the same one. I've seen you and him together before… I must know, is Michael in some kind of trouble?"

"Michael?" Julie asked, puzzled. "Oh! You mean Bruce, don't you? Well... I promised him I wouldn't say anything, but I wish I had never made that promise!" Tears formed in her eyes and she quickly wiped them away.

Mrs. Mayweather guided Julie to one of the study rooms and closed the door.

"Tell me everything," she said.

Julie left the library around four-thirty that afternoon after telling Mrs. Mayweather everything she knew about Bruce's situation. At one point Mrs. Mayweather started weeping. She had known things were not going well for Bruce, but had no idea that things were in such a desperate state. Together they formed a plan to help him and to take him out of that situation altogether.

Mrs. Mayweather was going to call the police and leave an anonymous tip that she suspected domestic violence at the Weber household. That would at least put them on alert if anyone called about shouting or fighting at the house.

Meanwhile, Julie was tasked with searching the internet for local organizations where they could get help for him. Failing that, she was to look up the national organizations that could aid them from the list Mrs. Mayweather provided.

Julie found a number of resources online about domestic violence and even a few organizations right there in Riverside. They were mostly for battered women, so she only found three that also focused on the kids. Two of those dealt exclusively with teenage victims of abuse. She took down the information and saved the numbers in her cell phone. At least she had someone to call if she saw that Bruce was in danger again. If those places could not help she also printed off information from the national organizations. She hoped it wouldn't come to that – they may take Bruce away – but she wanted to be prepared just in case.

She learned a lot about what to look for as well. Some of the signs of abuse that she found at the Mayo Clinic's website were changes in behavior including aggression and defiance, avoidance of authority figures, absences from school, and withdrawal from friends. Julie had noticed all of these in Bruce over the years and never paid any attention. There was information on the types of behavior the abuser exhibits, too, such as blaming the child for problems, describing the child in negative terms, and improper expectations of being cared for by the child. Julie had never seen Mr. Weber display any of these signs, but then again, she hadn't seen him in years.

She also found out there is such a thing as emotional abuse. She had never heard of that before so she spent some time finding out exactly what emotional abuse was and how to spot it in others. Low self-esteem and self-worth, social withdrawal, frequent headaches or stomachaches without cause, and a negative outlook were all symptoms of emotional abuse. Julie checked out another webpage as well and discovered that there were many different forms of emotional abuse including rejection, terrorizing, and isolating. She wondered how many of these signs were there the entire time and yet she never noticed. The agony that her friend must have gone through all these years! And it could have been stopped!

She visited one more page where she wrote down the steps for reporting abuse in her state. There were several documents that she printed and took with her as well, so she could read them over again. The most important thing she learned was that it was *not* up to her to conduct an investigation; that was for the authorities, including social workers and psychologists. Her *only* job in a suspected abuse case was to report it. She felt much better after learning that it was alright to report a *suspected* case; she didn't have to be certain. All in all, her search for information went very well after she opened up to Mrs. Mayweather.

She went home with a lighter heart now that she had someone with which to share this burden. It occurred to her that God had answered her prayers again without her ever needing to do anything. She was always amazed at how well He provided for her needs before she even knew them. She knew she could never doubt how much He loved her. *And Bruce...* she thought, *He loves Bruce that much, too. That's why He sent Mrs. Mayweather to help me. How wonderful You are, Lord!*

Julie even laughed as she thought of how things were falling into place. She believed with all her heart that things were going to be okay for him now. What she didn't realize was that things were going to get worse for her.

When Julie came home that day she found her mother home early and pacing in the kitchen.

"What's wrong, Mom?" Julie asked.

"Jo hasn't come home yet. I went by the school when she didn't call to tell me she was home, but all the kids had left already. Did you see her walking home?"

"No, I didn't pass her, but that doesn't mean she isn't

133

on her way. She could have taken a different route. Let's wait a bit longer before we jump to conclusions. It's only four forty-five. You know, she could have been held after school, too."

"Alright, but I'll only give her until five." Cynthia ceased her pacing and sat at the table, head in her hands.

Julie went over to give her mother a hug but before she could the doorbell rang.

When she opened the door a young girl she didn't recognize greeted her. She had beautiful flaming red hair and green eyes. Julie assumed this was Jo's friend Shauna.

"Hi, I'm Shauna. I was just checking on Jo since she wasna in school today. She missed a really big test, too. Is she well?"

"I think you'd better come inside, Shauna." Julie led her to the kitchen. "What do you mean Jo wasn't in school today, could you have passed each other and not seen her?"

"Och! No, we have three classes together and she wasna in enny of them. I guess that means she skipped... aye...? I'm sorry, I dinna mean ta —"

"No, no dear. Thank you for letting us know." Cynthia stood and patted Shauna on the shoulder. "You did a very good thing today. Do you need a ride home? I'm sure Julie would be glad to take you." She glanced at Julie with a look that spoke volumes.

"Sure would!" Julie said with a smile. "Say, did your mom happen to make cookies today?" Julie laughed to assuage some of Shauna's anxiety as they walked outside.

Shauna declined the ride since she lived just down the street, but she did promise to let her mom know that Julie would like some cookies next time she baked them.

Julie returned to the house to a very irate Mrs. Hathaway. She was on the phone with her husband and was clearly very angry with Johannah. She turned towards Julie when she heard her return.

"Julie, I want you to go down that *arcade* and bring that girl back here *now!*"

"Yes, Mom!" Julie had never seen her mother so worked up, but she knew she'd better hustle to the arcade. She dare not return without Jo, either!

But Jo wasn't at the arcade. She wasn't at the mall. She wasn't at the school. She wasn't at any of her friends' houses. Well, the ones Julie knew of anyway. Julie couldn't find her anywhere. Panic rose to the surface as she searched more and more places only to discover her sister could not be found.

Finally she returned home. Julie gathered her courage and walked in, desperately hoping that her sister was home.

She found her father pacing and her mother perched on the edge of the sofa seat, wringing her hands. They were right where they were supposed to be, home. All the pictures were there, the television was there, the stereo was there, the carpet and rugs were there, too. Everything was where it was supposed to be... except Jo. She wasn't there. Julie's panic rose even more, and a crease formed in her brow.

"I can't find her!" Julie said, "I can't find her anywhere, Mom! I can't find her!" She started to cry and her father came over to hold her close.

He didn't know what to say, none of them did. All they could do was wait and pray that she came home before too long. Should they call the police now or was it too soon? Julie didn't know the answer to that. She was frantically worried about her sister, as were her parents, but Jo has done this many times. What if it was another false alarm and they called the police for nothing? So many questions that Julie didn't have the answers to, just like with Bruce.

As the night passed their prayers went from praying that she would come home soon to praying that she would just come home…

The following morning brought no relief to Julie's exhausted and emotionally drained family. They still could not find Jo and she had not called. Cynthia told Julie to go to school, but there was no way Julie could concentrate on her lessons while her sister was missing. She said as much to her mother and Cynthia agreed to let her stay home.

They truly believed that Jo would come in around three in the morning like she has done before, but when she did not they rang the alarm. The police came to the house early that morning and started the search. Surprisingly, none of Julie's neighbors heard a thing. It wasn't until lunchtime that Neal called her cell to see where she was since she wasn't in the class they shared. Julie could not get through the call without bursting into tears and had to hang up.

She had never felt so helpless and afraid.

13

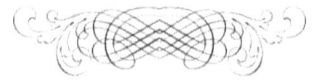

It had been three days, but his sides still ached and the bruises had only gotten more unsightly no matter how much ice he used. Bruce sighed and walked into Carson High on Friday morning. Of course, staying out late last night didn't help either.

As the morning passed, more and more people stopped to stare at his black eye and swollen lip. All the constant whispering and rumors of what happened only served to put him on edge and he quickly lost his temper. He lashed out at practically everyone, and by lunchtime no one dared come within ten feet of him.

Fine by me, he thought, *maybe I can get some peace and quiet now.* He grabbed his lunch and went to the library for some solitude. He passed Neal talking to someone on the phone. He heard him say Julie's name and ask where she was. *That's right, I haven't seen her today! Maybe she's sick, maybe she's avoiding me. She'd better be avoiding me! I can't let her get close, not till I'm ready to leave! And maybe not even then...*

He walked into the library and rounded the aisles to the back, his spot. He plopped down and munched on his chicken sandwich.

Come to think of it, he mused, *Julie never misses class... Maybe she really is sick? Could something have happened to her sister?* He ran his fingers through his hair – no longer spiky and dyed black but he couldn't say when he stopped doing it or why – and he went through several options in an attempt to determine why Julie was absent. A myriad of terrible things popped into and out of his mind and he lost track of time.

Mrs. Mayweather found him an hour and a half later, still leaning against the wall with a half-eaten chicken sandwich.

"Michael, why are you still sitting here – Oh my! What happened, my dear?" She rushed over to him and lifted his chin so she wouldn't have to kneel down beside him.

He wrenched his face away from her penetrating gaze and silently cursed himself for daydreaming.

"Nothin' alright? Just got in a fight. It happens. You should see the other guy, Mrs. M. I got 'im real good!" Bruce gathered the remains of his lunch and his books, but Mrs. Mayweather stopped him before he could rise and leave.

"I think we'll try the truth this time, hmm?" She fixed him with a stare she knew would force him into submission.

But Bruce was stronger than she estimated and simply stared right back as he stood up.

"Not your problem, Mrs. M. Let's keep it that way, you're the only one I can trust around here and I'd like it to stay that way."

"Yes, you can trust me, Michael. I know what's been happening at home. That young lady of yours came in here the other day looking up information on abuse and victimization. We pieced together—"

"*She did what?!?*" Bruce exploded. He stormed passed the stunned librarian and out into the hall.

I knew it! I knew she would blab! Now what's gonna happen? Will the police come? Will they question Dad at work? Oh man, this is bad! This is real bad! I gotta find her,

140

make her understand. But how? She's so infuriating! Think, Weber, think!

He wandered the halls completely preoccupied with figuring out his dilemma. When the bell rang signaling the end of sixth period some time later he had finally figured out what he was going to do, just as soon as she returned to school. He went to his next and final class of the day, but hardly paid any attention. His grade in this class was slipping – he'd only gotten an A- on the last quiz, something he was ashamed to admit – but he just couldn't focus when he believed his world was literally crashing down around him. He trusted her and look what happened? She betrayed his trust.

Never again, Weber, y'hear? Never trust anyone again. Finally, the bell rang and he could put this school day behind him. He stopped off at the library to apologize for his behavior to Mrs. Mayweather and finish off the last assignment before going home. He found his usual spot and had just sat down when The Trio, as he had dubbed them, came in and of course, sat at the table in the back.

I'm really getting sick of people picking that table, Bruce thought and got ready to leave. He had no intention of listening to them drone on again.

"...so the police are out looking for her and Jules is beside herself with worry," Neal said and finished his

141

brief recap of the conversation he had with Julie earlier.

Bruce stopped midstride and waited. *Something* did *happen! Sounds like Johannah...* Bruce mused. All thoughts of setting Julie straight vanished as he continued to eavesdrop on the conversation.

"I can't believe it, I just can't believe it!" Laurie was crying softly and shaking her head from side to side. "I never thought anything would *actually* happen to Jo! This is Riverside! Do you think she's been kidnapped? Have they called all of her friends?"

"Aye, that they did," Chris said. "Shauna came home and told us what happened yesterday. That Jo had skipped classes. They made an announcement in her class today that Jo had gone missing and if ennyone saw her to call the police right away. The police issued and Amber Alert an' ev'rythin'. I had ta pick Shauna up from school and take her home early. She couldna make it through the day and she has been cryin' ever since." Chris shook his head and rubbed the stubble that was starting to grow back on his chin.

Bruce had heard enough through eavesdropping. He approached the group and sat down.

They were shocked to see him, but he quickly jumped into their conversation.

"Jo's missing?" He asked, "I tried to warn them! I was

afraid something like this would happen. Tell me exactly what happened and what the Hathaway's have done so far." He turned to Neal as the designated leader of The Trio.

Neal was reluctant to offer anything to him, Bruce could tell. *Great, now I have to waste time convincing him to trust me.*

"Look, Julie told me about Jo a long time ago and I said I would see what I could find out. I knew she went to the arcade a lot so I decided to follow a hunch. I found out that her 'new friends' are part of a *very* bad gang and they go around recruiting kids from all over to join them. I told her folks not that long ago. We don't have much time if they took her, but I think I know where to start looking. I can't do that if you don't trust me now."

"Alright, we'll trust you," Neal replied and started retelling the story from the beginning. When he was finished the group sat, silently contemplating the events and a possible course of action.

"Thanks, I got the information I need." Bruce rose from the table and started walking away.

"Wait, what are you going to do? We should let the police handle this!" Laurie set aside her sobbing long enough to reveal her determination to stop Bruce from going vigilante.

143

"I'm solving this," Bruce said and left them wondering.

The Trio stared at each other for a brief moment, perplexed by his response, and then jumped up to chase after him.

"Hey, wait up," Neal called as Bruce sped up to avoid continuing the conversation. "Where are you going?"

"Yeah, wait up, we'll help!" Laurie, who was in better shape than the others, said as she caught up to Bruce. "You shouldn't do this alone, you could be killed!"

"No great loss," Bruce replied, and kept walking. They were outside now and he was almost to his bike. If he could just get there before the others finally caught up to him...

"*Every* life lost is a *tremendous* loss, Bruce," Laurie said. She grabbed his arm to slow him down and force him to wait for the others. "Besides, I have seen how you look at my best friend. *And* I have seen how she looks at you. It would be too great a loss if anything happened to you."

That brought him up short. *She looks at me a certain way?* Bruce thought. Whatever anger he still had towards Julie over revealing his secret disappeared as he pondered what Laurie could possibly mean by her statement. By this time Chris and Neal had caught up to

144

them and were listening intently.

"Yeah, whatever, so I care about Julie," Bruce said and turned in the direction of his bike again. "Nothing can ever come of it, so it doesn't matter. She'll get over me."

"I don't think so, Bruce. Not this time," Laurie said. "She really cares about you and would never forgive herself for saying anything at all if you get hurt because you went off after Jo. At least come with us to Julie's house. Get more information. We can't stop you–"

"Not sure we want to, anyway," Neal muttered under his breath.

"*But*," Laurie continued with a glare to Neal, "at least you won't go in ignorant of how this all came to pass."

"Yeah, fine, whatever," Bruce replied, "as long as it gets you off my back."

As Bruce drove to Julie's house he considered all the places Jo could have gone, or where she had been taken. The thought of her being taken against her will disturbed him greatly. What kind of people were they? Why would they recruit kids, especially young girls, from all around the country? What were they after? He had heard about human trafficking, he knew it was serious, but could they really be in his hometown? Actually working their horrid business in Riverside? The thought terrified him.

He remembered the research he had done last year for his final project in one of his social studies classes. They were given the opportunity to study one serious social issue in depth and write a report for the class. The teacher thought it would help the students prepare for what they may face in the future. Bruce didn't believe he would ever come across trafficking so he chose that one, figured it was an easy A.

He learned that there were groups, called rings, in America and that most people never even realized they were being scouted by traffickers. Many rings targeted young girls, but also young boys, between eleven and fourteen because they were prized by vile, perverted people, so traffickers knew that they would get top dollar. They would also be in the business longer than a thirty-year-old woman, so they could be marketed longer. He sincerely hoped this wasn't one of those rings. He theorized about how a ring would trap a young girl. How on earth could she not know she was in danger? Then Bruce remembered what Jake had told him; the MacPherson Gang uses young people to buddy up to unsuspecting kids. *That must be how they do it! They use kids to get kids! The older ones pretend to be interested in you and want you to join their group. Because you're a young teen or preteen you want to be accepted. They get you to rebel against your parents little by little over time so that when you disappear everyone thinks you've run away. Then, when you are the most trusting of them – maybe after a huge fight with your parents and you run to your new friends for comfort – they promise to take you to a "special" place where you can do whatever you want; no restricting rules or parents that will tell you you're being reckless. But really they just kidnap you and sell you to the highest bidder for who knows what purpose...* Bruce was angry, really angry. He had to find Jo and fast!

His best guess was that old warehouse downtown with the two guards, but he'd never get in there unnoticed. He needed a way to find Jo before they shipped her off, but without being seen. He knew he could be killed – Laurie didn't have to mention that at all – but he also knew if someone didn't stop these guys and fast more kids would be sold into slavery, either by making them prostitute themselves or turning them into mail-order-brides.

He had discovered from his research last year that there were trafficking rings that literally boxed women up and shipped them overseas to men that had "purchased" a bride through the mail. Bruce didn't want to think about what happened to those poor girls once

147

they were placed in that tiny box. He wondered how many arrived dead from starvation or lack of oxygen, and what the living ones lives were like when that box was opened.

The more he remembered from his research the more concerned he became for Jo and whoever else these people had taken. He had to figure out the best way to get to her and free her. He also knew from his studies that most kidnapped kids were moved out of the city within forty-eight hours, sometimes even within twenty-four hours. Jo had been missing since yesterday, but he didn't know what time she left the Hathaway house.

He pulled up in Julie's driveway just as the others were getting out of Neal's SUV. They must have taken a different route or he was going too slowly while musing about the danger Jo was in, because he really thought he would be the first to arrive.

They all took a moment to gather themselves before walking around to the back door. Between Neal's and Julie's houses, Neal turned around and grabbed Laurie's hand.

"Dear Lord," he began. Bruce took the opportunity to keep on walking. *Don't want none of that Christian stuff. Never helped me before, ain't gonna help now.* He noticed that Chris had stopped though, and joined hands with Neal and Laurie. *Great the whole lot of 'em are crazy! What have I gotten myself into now? Can't stop to think about that, though, Jo needs help.* He waited by the back door, but Neal just passed by him and opened it. Bruce had wondered why they came around back instead of ringing the doorbell, now he knew. *Wow, these Hathaway's got a lotta trust for these guys... Wonder what that's like...*

He entered to find Julie's parents pacing in the kitchen, Dr. Hathaway was on the phone as well, recapping what happened to whomever was on the other end. Laurie just pointed upstairs and Mrs. Hathaway simply nodded. She grabbed another tissue and wiped her eyes, her mascara had run down her cheeks, but she didn't seem to notice. *I remember my mom crying like that when Tom died. She never cried like that for me, she hated me...*

Bruce wished more than ever before that he could have known a life like Julie's during his teen years, instead of the mess he had created for himself by disappointing his parents to the point where they either left or drank. Would he ever know peace again? He vowed to himself to be a better husband and father to his own family if he should ever have one. He wasn't even

149

sure he wanted one, but he would do right by them like Dr. Hathaway.

He had a momentary flash of Julie holding their newborn baby in her arms, smiling up at him, his wedding band on her finger. A whisper in his mind said, *"This is what I have for you, Michael, if you let Me."* He was so startled by the vision and voice that he stumbled up the first few stairs.

"Ye alright, then?" Chris asked.

"Yeah, yeah, just keep moving," Bruce replied. He shook his head to clear it, but he couldn't shake the thought that something beyond his comprehension just happened.

They mounted the top of the stairs and turned down the hall to Julie's room. Laurie knocked softly on the door, and when Julie responded she whispered to the others that she would go in first but let them in if Julie allowed. *Why not just walk in?* Bruce thought, and he must have looked confused because Neal answered his unspoken question right away.

"It's improper for us as guys to just walk into Julie's bedroom without permission and without another girl or her parents present. It would compromise Julie's honor and integrity. Get it?"

No he did not get it. *Must be some strange Christian*

thing, weirdos... he thought. Still, he waited. After a few moments Laurie opened the door again and they all filed in to Julie's room, door left open.

Julie was sitting cross-legged on the bed wearing sweatpants and a long-sleeved tee shirt with a fleur-de-lis embroidered on the front. Her hair was down and with the sunlight streaming through the window creating highlights Bruce was mesmerized. He had never seen her look so beautiful, or so sad. Chris and Neal sat on the floor, but Bruce grabbed the desk chair and flipped it around so that he was straddling the chair. He rested his arms on the back and waited for someone to say something. They were all looking at him.

"Uh-huh," he cleared his throat and started again. "Hey Hathaway, we just came to see how you were holding up and find out exactly what happened. I noticed you weren't in school, but I had no idea all this was going down. Tell me everything."

Julie looked at him with such sadness in her eyes that his own misted up, just a little. He rubbed his face to hide his tears, but he knew she saw.

"Jo is missing. She didn't go to school yesterday, but we don't know exactly when she disappeared. I was so concerned with your situation that I completely forgot to check on her before I left yesterday morning. Mom

151

and Dad had already gone, so Jo would have been left here alone until it was time for her to go to school. She's used to it and we've never had any problems before, I mean, it's Riverside, but now..."

14

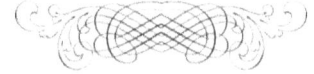

Julie retold the story for what seemed like the thousandth time, but this time Bruce – no, Michael, she was going to call him Michael from now on – was there. She knew, she just *knew*, that she could make it with him there. She wouldn't break down *this* time. The look he gave her as he asked after her melted her heart, and she knew the tears were real. *He really does care for me, doesn't he...?* Julie thought as she paused in her story.

"Wait," Neal interrupted, "what situation with Bruce?"

"Nothing," he replied. "Stay out of it." He gave Neal

such a fierce look that for a moment Julie wondered if she imagined his tenderness of a moment ago. *He must really want to keep that whole mess private... Can't say I blame him, I don't want anyone knowing about our situation, but we both need help right now. It's no time for pride!*

Julie kept her eyes fixed on Michael as she told her friends what had transpired since her mother noticed Jo's absence. Somehow she was able to draw strength from his steady gaze. His eyes implored her to stay focused on him and she had no intention of doing otherwise. She gave them as much detail as she could about her search the previous day and what the authorities had done so far, but it all seemed so hopeless. Her sister could be anywhere! She may not even be in Riverside anymore! What would they do if Jo was taken to some other city or country? She knew human traffickers were in the United States, but surely these new friends of Jo's weren't traffickers! Were they...?

Michael said they came from a larger organization in Chicago, and she knew the Midwest was a common stop for traffickers. The thought sickened Julie and she laid her head down on Laurie's lap. The tears flowed again just as soon as she broke eye contact with Michael. Laurie just stroked her hair and whispered soothing words to her. Julie could hear the sharp intake of breath from Michael's side of the room, but she couldn't see who it was. It could just as easily have been Chris or Neal.

"Aw, Jules," Neal started, "I wish there was something we could do to help." He handed her a tissue and sat back down. "Could there be any chance that she just stayed at one of her friends' houses all this time. You know, a rebellion against being sent away?"

"No, I doubt it. She *is* still really upset with Mom and Dad over shipping her off to Sioux Falls after Christmas, and she ran away to avoid it, I'm sure of it. But where? She should be back by now if she just stayed at a friend's house. The police said Jo is the fifth girl to go missing in the past six months! This is Riverside! These things don't happen here! They assure us that the incidents are probably not connected, but I know better. It's those new friends of hers, isn't it, Michael?" Julie looked over to him and saw the confirmation in his eyes. He stood to leave instead of replying, but she stopped him.

"Where are you going? I know you too well, Michael." She paused and considered all she knew of this young man that had somehow changed her life. "You're going after her, aren't you? You're going to search for Jo!"

"Yeah, what of it?" Michael switched his weight from one foot to the other, his nervousness evident, but Julie wasn't going to throw him a lifeline this time. She rose and walked over to him. This time she needed him to see reason, to stop him from possibly getting himself – and maybe even Jo – killed. She had to stop him!

"You can't go! What if something happened to you? At least let me come with you, Michael, please!" Julie started to wring her hands and a crease formed between her brows.

"Absolutely not! I would die if anything happened to you! Listen, I will be careful, I promise, but we don't have time if they really are traffickers. They could ship her off to who-knows-where at any moment. I'm willing to bet they have her in that warehouse I told you about. Don't worry about me, JuJu," he paused and kissed the top of her head before continuing softly. "It's no great loss if anything happens to me." He turned to leave again, but she stopped him and turned him to face her. She reached up and wrapped her arms around his neck.

"It would be to me," she whispered.

She held on tight in an effort to make him realize how much she cared for him, too. She loved the little nickname he had given her. No one had ever called her that before, and she noticed he didn't correct her for using his real name, not even once. She just didn't see him as Bruce anymore, now that she knew his turmoil.

No, she couldn't bear it if anything happened to him, not when he was finally opening up and trusting someone again. She knew they could help him get out of his situation, and maybe he would return to his old self if they could, but if he ran off now…

"Please, Mike," she whispered in his ear, and nestled against his neck. "Don't go. Stay here with me. I need your strength right now. Please…"

He just held on to her tightly and brushed the softest of kisses in her hair. "I have to," he whispered and kissed her hair again. He released her and rushed out of her room and down the stairs. Before she could react she heard his motor start and then he was gone. She hugged herself and slowly the tears began to fall again. This time for the man she had begun to love and may end up losing by the end of the night. She couldn't bear anymore sadness. Why didn't he listen?

She turned and walked over to her bed again. She looked up to the flabbergasted looks on her best friends' faces.

"Um," Laurie began.

"Mind telling us," Neal continued.

"What just happened?" Chris finished.

As the hours passed Julie's friends stayed by her side

and prayed. Dr. Hathaway ordered a few pizzas, but no one felt like eating. The police called with updates and the grandparents checked in every hour on the nose. The waiting was agonizing, but it was all they could do. They had tried everywhere and called everyone they knew.

Mrs. Hathaway just rocked slowly back and forth, forth and back, and occasionally would burst into tears. Her hands were red from all the squeezing and twisting as she worried. Dr. Hathaway just paced down the hall and back again. Julie sat and hugged a pillow. She would sniffle every now and then, too, a nervous habit she had developed as a child that only manifested itself when she was extremely worried. Everyone was completely consumed with thinking about Johannah. Julie was probably the only one that spent more time praying for Mike, though.

She had finally broken through his barriers and reached the hurting young man inside, and now he was out there somewhere risking his life to find a little, headstrong girl who had been manipulated by some of the most evil people in the world. How could something like this have happened to their perfect little family? Maybe that was it; she knew Satan sought to steal, kill, and destroy. It was only a matter of time before he targeted her family in an attempt to destroy them. He targeted all Christians, no one was left alone. Satan despised her and others like her. *Well,* she thought, *I'd rather be targeted by Satan than to be left alone by him.*

She called everyone together and shared her thoughts. She asked if they could all pray together instead of apart like they had been. She knew there was power in prayer and especially in joining *together* in prayer. Mrs. Hathaway looked up for the first time in hours and truly focused on her surroundings.

"You're right, honey," she said. "You are absolutely right! I have been worrying instead of truly praying as I know I should. Jesus instructed us not to worry, and the Bible says to make our requests known to the Lord, but I haven't done either. Come, let us all pray together."

Neal, Laurie, Chris, Julie, and her parents all clasped hands and started to pray. When it was Julie's turn in the circle she added a special spoken prayer for Michael, "Please, Lord, keep Michael safe as he searches for Jo. Send him help and protection. Blind the eyes of those that would seek to harm him and Jo. Please bring them both safely back to me."

Next in the circle was Chris and his simple prayer impacted everyone present, "Lord Jesus, thank You for bringing me and my family out of Ireland and the hard situation we faced there. Thank You for helping us ta find people that truly love You in our new home. I didna think it was possible ta find a group o' true believers after what we have been through but You sent us here ta Riverside and brought each of these people inta our lives ta show us Your love and how You have preserved us for something greater. I was angry with You at first for sending us away from a land that I love, but now I see Your greater purpose. Your plan for us and for the friends You have given us. We are ta help each other and stand united against the evil one. Please, Lord, bring Jo safely home. Keep Bruce safe, too, and send him aid at just the right moment. Help us all ta be strong when they do come home, and I have faith that You will bring them home."

Neal was the last in the circle and so closed the prayer, "Lord, please bless each person present here and all those that are praying for Jo around the world. Help her see where she went wrong so that this never has to happen again. Please bring justice in a way only You can for the other girls that are missing and their families. Please Lord, bring them *all* safely home. We know that You are with Jo and Bruce even now and are guiding their steps. We leave them in Your hands and praise You for all that you have done for us. Thank you, Lord Jesus. Amen."

Just then the back door opened and Julie's older brother Josh came in. She ran to him and threw her arms around him.

"Josh! You're home! We didn't know you were coming!"

"How could I not be here? My baby sis is missing! I came as fast as I could." The door opened again and in walked David with a few duffle bags. Laurie hurried over to him and gave him a hug.

"I drove JC over here when I heard Johannah was missing. I wanted to be here for you all, too. You're like family," he said and reached over to give Julie a hug. "How are you doing, Julie?"

"Much better now that everyone I care about is here. Well, almost everyone…" she trailed off, her thoughts on Mike and Jo. David just hugged her again and then went to move their bags into Josh's old room.

"Aye, that He does, my friend, that He does," Chris finished. At Julie's look of confusion Neal filled her in on their conversation.

"I was just telling Chris that when the Lord moves, He *moves*! Look what the Lord has done for us before we even finished praying!"

"That's true! Now we have even more people to join us in praying and Josh gets to be here when Jo walks through that door!"

For the first time since Jo disappeared Julie had hope again.

15

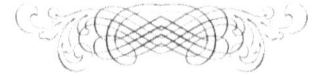

Bruce hurried out of that house as fast as he could before he compromised his vow to keep Julie out of harm's way. He hadn't meant to kiss her, let alone kiss her several times! But somehow, it just felt natural. She didn't pull away, either. She even nestled closer to him. He so desperately wanted to be worthy of her, but he knew he could never hope for a blessing such as her. He was irredeemable and always would be, his mistakes saw to that. There was no forgiveness for someone like him.

He got on his bike and drove to the arcade first. He didn't think they were there, but maybe Jake was and he could get a little more information before heading to the warehouse. At least Jake would be able to tell the authorities when they found Bruce's dead body. *No,* he thought, *Michael. It's time. I like it better. Always hated 'Bruce' anyway.* But he wouldn't let anyone else call him Mike. That was just for JuJu. He was glad she liked the nickname. Well, she didn't stop him anyway. He had thought of her as JuJu for a long time, but never had the courage to use it. He chose to call her Hathaway instead; better for keeping his distance. Maybe, if he could save Jo, he could hope to be her friend, but that was all. He may never get the chance to call her JuJu again, but he hoped he could. *At least one more time when I deliver her sister, alive and well*, he mused.

He pulled into the arcade parking lot and went inside. He didn't see Jake, so he called and left a message on his cell. Maybe Jake would call him back before he got to the warehouse. He didn't say much, just that he was following a lead on the Hathaway girl and was heading to the warehouse to find her. He figured that would get Jake's attention and he'd call pretty quick.

He didn't tell him that he also planned on confronting the kidnappers, if that's what they were, and stopping them once and for all from taking anyone else's baby girl. He had seen how deeply this affected Julie and her family, her friends, too. He had never experienced anything like it, not that he could remember anyway. He knew there were families out there in a better state than his and he didn't want anyone else to suffer as he had, as the Hathaway's were suffering now. He decided right then and there to change his intended major to social work instead of business. It wouldn't make him as much money, but he would be doing some good in the world. Helping people get out of bad situations may just earn him the privilege of contacting Julie again someday. It wouldn't redeem him, nothing could, but it would help.

Man, she felt good in my arms, he mused. He had about a ten minute drive to the warehouse district and he couldn't keep his mind from wandering back to Julie and how amazingly wonderful it felt to hold her again. He still couldn't believe she initiated the hug this time and it wasn't because she was nearly mugged. She wanted him to know she cared what happened to him. She *cared!* She held him close and nestled against him to show him she *cared*. He still couldn't believe it. Oh how he loved that girl! And oh how he hated himself for messing up so badly that he could never hope to be with her.

He waited at a traffic light and again the image of Julie holding their newborn came to him. Again he heard

165

the voice in his head saying, *"I have this for you, if you let Me."* Again, he ignored it as his own wild imagination. This time was different, though. This time he felt a distinct sadness as he dismissed the idea and committed himself to his course. A sadness, but there was still a determination, too. He couldn't explain it. It didn't *feel* like it came from him, but it had to. No one else was there.

He arrived at the warehouse around five thirty only to find it deserted. *Wait, where are they? I thought for sure they would be here!* Michael looked around anxiously for any signs that the warehouse wasn't abandoned but it was. Devastated, he sat down at the curb near his bike and laid his head in his hands. His chance to do what was right was gone. His chance to start earning the right to be Julie's friend faded away. He was so certain that they would be there! Why else post a guard at a dilapidated old warehouse? He wracked his brain for another location to try, but came up with nothing. *God, if you're real would You throw me a line? Anything would be great.* He didn't really believe in God, but Julie did. Maybe, just maybe, if God was real, He'd be willing to help him find Jo. Just then his phone chirped. He thought it was Jake returning his call, but it was Matt instead.

166

"Hey buddy! Jake told me you were keeping an eye on that gorgeous girl's sister for her, right? About eleven, strawberry blonde hair? Yeah, so a buddy of mine, lives just outside of town on the west side, called and said he saw someone that looked about like that in a van with a couple other kids. They drove to the old abandoned farm near his house, and he said they all looked like they'd been crying. So yeah, the van had Illinois plates and he thought it was odd. I told him to call the cops, but I don't know if he did. Anyway, thought you should know! You may want to call your girl. Something might have happened. Later!"

God heard me? Couldn't be. Just coincidence. Michael knew just what farm Matt was talking about and hopped back on his bike. He had to hurry before they moved again! It would take him at least an hour to traverse the city and get to the other side, and that's if there was no traffic. He had to get there in time, he just *had* to!

Michael arrived at the farm around eight. There was a *lot* of traffic that night. He supposed people were heading out of town for the weekend. He cut the engine and left his bike about five hundred yards from the farmhouse. Hopefully no one heard him pull up. He crouched beside a rock and observed the farmhouse for a few minutes while he thought up a game plan. He could

167

just go up to the front door and knock, but he supposed that wouldn't accomplish his goals. What if they were armed? He didn't have any weapons with him and couldn't successfully fight off more than two attackers, one if they were armed. His training hadn't progressed that far yet. How to get in there and find Jo? His phone chirped again and he jumped. He fumbled around trying to silence it and wished he had left it turned off back at his bike.

"Hello!" he hissed into the phone.

"What on earth do you think you're doing!?" Jake yelled on the other end. "Get back here now before you get yourself *killed*!"

"I'm not in town anymore, Jake," he replied. "I can't go back. Not until I find Jo."

"I know you're not in town," Jake said. "I'm parked next to your bike. Get over here!"

Michael crept back to his bike and sure enough, there was Jake's beat up old junker. *How did he find me?* Michael wondered. He didn't have long to wonder though, Jake answered his unspoken question as soon as he walked up.

"Matt called. Said he thought you'd be stupid enough to come out here after what he told you." Jake shook his head. "Let me guess, you were trying to figure out how to get in there, right?"

Michael nodded. "Well yeah, but I hadn't figured out a way that didn't get me all shot up, you know?"

Jake just shook his head. "Look, I know this place. Used to hang out here. There's a cellar in the back behind a bunch of dried up bushes. That will let you into the basement unless they secured it somehow. Might just get you in and out without anyone noticing you." Jake had gotten quieter as he spoke, as if he was no longer talking to Michael but to himself. "Stay here, I'll check it out first."

As he got out of the car Michael struck him on the back of the head, effectively knocking him out for a while. "Sorry, buddy. Can't let you get killed on my account. You'll understand later." He went to his bike and sent a quick text to Jake, then started towards the back of the farmhouse. "I hope anyway…"

He found the cellar just as Jake described and it was unlocked and unguarded. He very slowly opened the creaking door and hoped no one could hear it. He took his time so that the creaking would appear random just in case. About five minutes later he finally got the door open and stepped down into the basement. It was dark so he gave himself a moment for his eyes to adjust. He heard whimpering from somewhere ahead and to his right. He quietly went in that direction, feeling his way in front of him. Several times he bumped into objects and had to stop and listen. So far no one above had noticed him. *Or they ain't movin' if they did...* he mused. He couldn't worry about that now, right now he needed to see where that whimper was coming from. He hoped it was Jo. It just *had* to be Jo! He had a tiny flashlight in his back pocket. He had grabbed it from the compartment on his bike before heading to the house, but he dared not use it. What if there was a guard down here just waiting for him to make a mistake like that?

The whimpering was getting closer. It was still to his right... Wait, it was also in front of him. There! Another whimper! Michael was sure there were two distinct sounds now. And again to his left! Three! There were at least three people down here crying! *Now what...* he thought to himself. He couldn't just leave them all here. He wouldn't! No one deserved this! He scuttled over to the closest sound and whispered very quietly, "Can you talk? I'm here to get you all out of here. How many of you are there?"

Only a muffled noise escaped from the captive. He whispered that he was going to search for a gag and gently touched the person in front of him. He found the gag, but before he removed it he elicited a promise that the young girl – he was sure it was a young girl now, with long hair – would not cry out or make any noise to alert them all of his presence.

"There are three of us down here and we're alone. The guards leave us all alone down here!" She started to cry, but she was true to her word, she did so quietly.

"Ok, I'm going to get you out, but you have to do as I say, alright?"

"Okay," she whimpered. "I'm Jo Hathaway. Can we call my mom and dad?"

"Jo!" Michael couldn't believe his luck! He went straight to the right girl! "Jo! I'm a friend of Julie's. My name is Michael. I'm so glad I found you!" He reached out and hugged her close. He noticed she didn't hug him back though and felt around to see how she was bound. She was tied hands and feet to a post or support beam. He undid her bindings and she grabbed hold of him tightly.

"Oh thank you, thank you, thank you! Take me home! I want to go home!" She continued to cry, but she also kept her promise.

"I have to get the others. Wait right here!"

Michael approached the two other girls in the basement and untied them. They removed their own gags and stayed as quiet as they could. Michael told them to hold hands and he led them back to the cellar door.

"Jo, my buddy Jake has a car about five hundred yards that way," he said and pointed. "I want you to run to it, d'ya hear me? Run! Jake will take care of you and take you home, I promise. You can trust him."

Jo just held onto his waist and shook her head. "No, no! You have to come too! Don't leave me, please!"

He held her close and knelt down. He took her hands and placed them in each of the other girls' hands. "They need you to be strong, can you do that? Lead them to Jake. I know you can do this, you're a Hathaway!" When she nodded in the moonlight, he knew she would follow through.

"I'm just going to make sure no one else is down here. I don't want to leave *anyone* behind. I'll be right there, okay?" She nodded again and still holding hands all three girls ran in the direction he pointed. He watched them until they disappeared from view and then turned to search the rest of the basement.

He didn't get far when the light came on and three men wrestled him to the ground. He fought as best he could, but there were one too many for him to handle. The blows rained down as he struggled to gain a footing. If he could just get to his feet again he might –

WHACK!!! A fourth man had come up behind him and

172

hit him hard with a bat. His world went dark. He came to sometime later with his hands bound behind him and a gag in his mouth. He heard voices upstairs discussing what to do with him and where their captives could be.

Good! They got away! Michael didn't care what happened to him now. Jo was safe at last! Now Julie wouldn't cry anymore. He never wanted her to cry again. He hurt in places he didn't know he had and he was extremely nauseous. He must have had a concussion. *Of course I have a concussion! I was hit over the head with a bat!* He could also tell his ribs were broken, his wrist was broken, and possibly his ankle. He tried moving his leg but stopped suddenly. *Yup! It's broken! How am I going to get out of here now...?*

First he had to untie himself. Not a difficult task, one his martial arts teacher had taught him long ago, but he wasn't so sure with a broken wrist. He shifted one way and then another until he had gotten free of his bonds. His wrist was very swollen and in excruciating pain, but he had to get free. He'd worry about the damage later. He released his hands and went to work on his feet. Freeing himself after several minutes of intense pain and the heroic strength to avoid crying out, he gingerly crawled to the cellar door.

It was locked. He pulled out the flashlight now, not

caring who saw it. Jo was safe. That was all that mattered. He found an open window not far from his position and crept over to it. They must have left it open for ventilation, trusting their ability to tie knots over posting a guard. *Foolish*, he thought. He had to stand on his broken ankle, but he made it through the window and outside. He belly crawled the distance back to his bike and noticed that Jake's car was gone. He started the motor; he didn't care if they heard, he had to get away from there. Behind him he heard the sounds of gunfire and shouting, but he couldn't worry about that now. He had to move and *fast!* He made it about halfway back to his house before the pain became unbearable. He blacked out and skidded off the road.

16

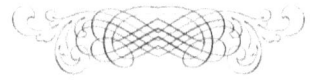

Jo raced up the street to her house and ran inside. She immediately found her mother and fell into her arms. "Mommy! Mommy! Mommy!" Jo cried and cried, repeating the word over and over again.

"My baby! My baby! You're home! Are you alright? My baby!" Mrs. Hathaway just held her little girl close and rocked her back and forth, the tears streaming down her face. Dr. Hathaway joined them, and then Julie, and then Josh, and suddenly everyone was hugging everyone and praising God that Jo was home! Oh the joy Julie felt when she saw her sister race through the door! She was stunned at first and thought it was her imagination, but no she was real! Jo was home!

As the hug lessened and her friends pulled away Julie looked for Michael. She was sure he was standing in the background, giving them their moment. She looked for him, but didn't find him.

"Julie," Jo said. "Your friend, Michael, he saved me! But you have to go back! He never met us at the car. He said he would but he didn't! He never came! You have to go back! He's hurt, I know it! He saved me!" Jo was rambling on and the tears wouldn't stop, but Julie got the message. Something had happened to Michael.

"Start at the beginning, Jo," she said. "The very beginning. Why did you skip school?"

As her mom and dad held Johannah close, she told them everything that had happened since she decided to skip school. She told them about her new friends and how they convinced her that her parents just wanted to hurt her, that they didn't care about her at all, and how she should just leave home for good. At this her parents shook their heads, adamantly denying the claims that they didn't care.

"I know, Mama, I know," Jo said. "But they made it sound so believable! They made it sound like the truth! I didn't even realize what was happening until it was too late. I went to the arcade and told them that I was being

176

shipped off and they said it was time to show me the funhouse. The place where they all hung out every day. They told me that they had all run away from home and that I could join them if I wanted. At the time, I really wanted to leave home... I went with them. But they lied, Daddy! They lied!" Jo burst into a fresh set of tears, but she was determined to continue. "They gave me a drink that made me sleepy and they tied me up! When I woke up I was in a van and I didn't know where they were taking me! This man was there and he said such awful things... He said he found a *buyer* for me and he was getting a lot of money to send me to him. He was going to ship me in a box to Kansas City and then to Mexico. From there he said the man would meet me and take me someplace else..." Jo stopped and started hiccoughing. Laurie went to the kitchen and got a glass of water for her. Jo thanked her and took a huge gulp.

"Daddy," she turned to her father. "What did he mean? What was that man going to do?"

Dr. Hathaway didn't have the heart to tell her the truth, not yet, so he simply said he didn't know. But they all knew. The horrible truth of Jo's story hit all of them right between the eyes.

"If Michael hadn't gotten to you in time..." Julie started, but couldn't finish. The tears pooled in her eyes and she couldn't hear any more about what had almost befallen her baby sister. "Jo, tell me what happened to Michael."

"He crawled into the basement where we – there were three of us – were being held and untied us. He told us to run to his friend Jake and he would be right behind us. He wanted to make sure no one else was down there. But he never came, Sis!" Jo was anxious for her new hero and rose to go to the door. "We have to go back! We have to find him! He saved me! He could be hurt!"

"No Jo," Neal said, "stay here with JC and your mom and dad. We will go find him, okay? You just stay here and rest." Neal gave a silent signal to the others and they all pitched in their agreement with him.

"Yes, Jo, stay here," Julie said. "I will bring him back, don't worry. What did this place look like?"

While Jo tried to recall where she was being held, Dr. Hathaway called the police to tell them Jo had been found and they were quick to arrive. Laurie, Neal, Chris, David, and Julie all piled into David's SUV since it could hold all of them, and drove out to the farmhouse Jo described.

"I know that place," David said as he pulled out of the driveway. "It was a favorite hangout for the football team when I was in high school." At Laurie's glare, he clarified. "It was before you introduced me to Jesus, hon, don't worry. I don't do that stuff anymore, promise. Anyway, I know a back road that will get us to the edge of town faster. Shaves about half an hour off the trip."

But as they were driving Julie had a strong desire to head in a different direction.

"Wait!" Julie called. "Turn here! Hurry! Turn here!"

"Why, Jules?" Neal asked. "What's up? Do you see something?"

"No, but I know we *must* turn here. It's a feeling, a strong one!"

David turned down the street Julie indicated and about one hundred yards in front of them was a motorcycle on its side against a tree. David stopped the car and they all got out.

"It's his bike!" Julie ran to it and started calling Michael's name. When there was no answer they all fanned out to search for him.

Neal found him underneath some bushes not far from his bike. He called the others over and Julie reached them first.

"Mike? Mike? Can you hear me? We have to call an ambulance! He's hurt! Bad!" She saw the bruises and the odd shape of his wrist and ankle. Laurie called for an ambulance as Neal and Julie stayed beside Michael.

He opened his eyes briefly and saw Julie. "JuJu... My angel... here... I'm dead..." he said and fell back into unconsciousness.

Julie let the tears fall as she held him close. She whispered into his ear, "No, I'm not an angel, just a girl who loves you. Jo is safe, you did it. Now you just rest in my arms. I won't leave you."

The ambulance arrived and took him to the nearest emergency room. The others followed and waited for his prognosis in the hospital waiting room.

"I never thought I'd say this," Neal started, "but I hope he's okay. He made a friend for life in me today. He was willing to die for you and your sister, Jules. He made a friend for life..."

"Same here," Laurie said. "I will always be grateful to him for saving my little sister, and for loving my big sister, too." She was sitting next to Julie and wrapped an arm around her "big sister's" shoulder as she said it. The Hathaway's were her family, just as much as her own was, and she wanted to make sure Julie knew how much she cared for Jo, too. "He made a friend for life today."

"Same here," said David.

"Aye, me too," chimed in Chris.

The doctor arrived and told them that since Michael's father declined to appear, and granted them permission to "tell 'those darn kids' whatever you want" since he "wasn't going down there if you paid" him to, they had the authorization necessary to discuss his condition. He had several broken ribs, a broken wrist, one broken ankle and the other one was sprained, a severe concussion, a broken clavicle, and several lacerations and abrasions. The doctor said that since he was in excellent shape he should make a full recovery, but that his will to fight for his life must also be strong. His concussion could make him worse and they would keep him in the hospital until he regained consciousness.

Michael's new group of best friends stayed as long as he was in emergency, but when they admitted him to one of the rooms upstairs they had to leave.

David drove them all back to Julie's house where they filled her parents in on what happened. Jo had gone upstairs to sleep after the police were finished questioning her. When she told them about the other girls, though, they already knew. They weren't the same girls that went missing earlier. Those young girls were still missing; these two had not even been reported as missing yet. They said they had someone on the inside that informed them of the rescue long before Dr. Hathaway called.

Julie wondered who it could have been since she was pretty sure it wasn't Michael. Maybe that friend of his that brought Jo home? Whoever he was – or she – Julie was grateful and asked a special blessing for that person. In fact, Julie went to sleep asking that the Lord bless all the people that helped bring Jo home, and praising Him that she was found and returned to them. The last prayer on her lips was for a very special person lying in a hospital bed fighting for his own life.

Julie awoke early the next morning. She wanted to be at the hospital as soon as visiting hours started. She downed her coffee and toast quickly and stuffed her homework into her schoolbag so she would be able to do some of it while she waited for Michael to wake up. She peeked in on her sister before she left and for the first time was overjoyed to hear Jo's soft snoring. It meant she was home and sleeping peacefully. Oh, Julie knew Jo would have nightmares, how could she not? But Jo was among people who loved her and could protect her. Jo understood that now, and Julie was glad that she did. She would always be there for her little sister, always.

Julie arrived at the hospital just as visiting hours started and she stayed until visiting hours ended. She did that every day. Every single day for a solid week. Her friends brought her homework each afternoon and came every morning to get her completed assignments to turn in for her. With each day Julie grew more and more concerned, cried more and more for her Michael. Every single day for a week. And still Michael slept... The doctors said that he just didn't have the will to fight.

"This is what I have for you, if you let Me..." there it was again. He heard it clearly this time. The same voice as before. It wasn't his voice, it was Someone else's. The images were there, too, but there were more. He could see fuzzy pictures of a house and an office. Vague shadows of people he was helping. He wished he could see it more clearly this time, like he could hear the Voice in his head. Just at the edges of his mind he heard weeping.

Strange, he thought, *there wasn't weeping in all the others...* He followed the sound until he reached a stone wall. *What's this doing here...?* He pushed at the wall, but it wouldn't move. He looked around for a door, but there was none. He walked for a while in one direction and then the other, but there was no end to the wall. The sound was louder now, too. He had to get through this wall! Someone was crying! Someone needed his help! He pushed against the wall again and again, but it wouldn't fall. He kicked at the wall and punched the wall, but it wouldn't budge. Finally, he just gave up and leaned his head against the wall. He couldn't reach whoever was crying. *Wait a minute...,* he thought. *I know that sound... Where have I heard that before...? Julie!* He renewed his efforts to break the wall and gave it his strongest kick. The wall broke into pieces all around him. He closed his eyes to avoid all the dust.

When he opened them again he saw Julie, his JuJu, sitting next to his hospital bed crying. She held his hand and she was speaking.

"Please, Lord, help him wake up. It's been so long and he won't wake up! Please, Lord, show him the way out, and help him break down the walls that are blocking him from returning to us. Show him that you have a plan for him, Lord, and give him something to hope for, something to return to. Please... please..."

"JuJu?" His voice was rough and scratchy, like he hadn't spoken in days. He tried again, "JuJu, what's wrong? Why are you crying?" He reached for her, but was too weak. She looked up and he was certain her smile could light up the cosmos for millennia.

"You're awake! Oh, you're awake!" She leaned over him and gently hugged him. She peppered his cheek with her soft kisses and kept repeating the phrase over and over.

184

Her weight on his chest hurt, but he wasn't about to tell her to move. He wanted just the opposite in fact, for her to stay close to him always. At last, she withdrew and sat beside him again.

"I heard you crying, JuJu. I heard you. I had to get to you, but I couldn't. There was a wall in the way. You were crying... Who were you crying for?" Michael didn't want to believe, to hope, that it was for him. He didn't want to believe that she cared enough to pray for him. Not *him*!

"For you, silly! Yes, I was crying for you, and praying, too." She wiped her eyes with the back of her hand. "You've been asleep a long time. I was so worried!"

"How long?" Michael asked.

"A little over two weeks. Thanksgiving was two days ago. The first week I was here every day, but I couldn't miss any more school or work."

"What!? I was asleep *that long*?" He laid his head back, stunned at how much time he had missed.

"Jo!" He tried to sit up, but the pain was too great. He cried out and fell back into the pillows.

"Shhh... it's okay, she's fine. She and the other girls all made it safely home. They have been in counseling sessions this week and will continue to go to sessions for a long time, but they are home and they are safe. You did it! I don't know how to thank you, Mike, I really don't."

She held his hand and he used what strength he had left to squeeze her hand back. "You're doing it. Just stay with me a little longer. I just want to remember this moment, here with you. I know it can't last, but just for a little while..." he trailed off and closed his eyes. If he could just stay with her forever... but he knew he couldn't, strange dreams and all. He knew he was unworthy.

"What do you mean, Mike?" Julie asked. "This *can* last. If you want it to, that is..." she started to remove her hand from his but he wouldn't let go.

"I'm unworthy of you... irredeemable... the things I've done... I don't deserve you..." he was getting weaker by the moment, but he had to make her understand. Best to get the pain over with now rather than later, after she had invested too much.

"But, Mike," she started, but he cut her off.

"No, I understand. It has to be this way... But maybe, someday... I can earn the privilege of seeing you again... Maybe someday..." he trailed off again and it was harder to keep his eyes open. As the nurse entered to verify the readings that he was awake, he could fight no longer and fell asleep.

When he awoke again it wasn't Julie by his bedside,

it was Jake.

"Hey buddy!" Michael said. "I wasn't expecting to see you. Not after I decked you and all..."

"Yeah, well," Jake started. "I should have arrested you for that, but I didn't. Don't know why... you big dummy."

"Arrested me? What? I must still be hallucinating..."

"Nope. You're awake." Jake held out his hand. "Allow me to reintroduce myself, Detective Jacob Stearns, missing persons division. You nearly destroyed three years of hard work, you know."

Michael just stared at him. He suspected there was more to his friend, but a *cop*? "No way, I don't buy it."

Jake recited his credentials and brief history, essentially silencing further dispute. "Matt, too, but he was reassigned before you woke up. Said to tell you, 'Good job, Runt.'"

"No wonder you were a junior for three years... and here I thought you were just dumb... Huh," Michael responded.

"Gee, thanks, kid," Jake sat down next to him. "You really did scare me, you know. I never intended for you to go in there. I was going to knock *you* unconscious, instead you outsmarted me. As soon as I came to my senses again and realized you were in there I called for

187

backup. About a minute later three young girls ran up to the car. They said you were right behind them and we should wait for you, but there was movement on the premises. I took a huge risk and drove away before my backup arrived. That move could have gotten you killed! You should have let us handle it. What were you thinking?!?"

"I had to make sure no one else was being held there... It was awful, they had them tied up like... like... I don't want to think about it."

"Yeah, well, I understand, but please," Jake said, "don't ever scare me like that again, okay? I have come to think of you as a little brother these past three years, kid. I thought you were dead..."

"I'm sorry." And Michael meant it. He was sorry for a lot of things lately. "What happened after you left?"

"I notified dispatch and told them to hustle, that you were still in there. You know how it is, paperwork... Waiting for so-and-so to submit such-and-such before the judge can sign the order and return it to so-and-so so that you can finally go in guns blazing... Takes time, and we were almost ready when you ran in headfirst! When the girls found me I told the team to move *now* to get you out, but when the SWAT team arrived you were gone. They did round up the trafficking ring, though. You stalled them just long enough for that, but no one could find you, or your corpse. I hightailed it back to the farmhouse and joined the search for your body. That's when the call came over the radio that you had been found by some teens and taken to the hospital. I've never been so relieved… You really scared me, kid." Jake said again and shook his head.

"Hey," Michael said. "I'm really sorry. I am. I never meant to scare you. I thought I was keeping a lunkhead alive!" He chuckled and when Jake looked up he joined in.

"Yeah, okay, okay," Jake rose to leave. "Here, I saved this for you." He set an envelope within reach. Michael opened the envelope and inside was a stack of bills.

"I don't get it," he asked, "what's this?"

"All the money you gave me for information. I noticed you spent wildly and I was willing to bet you had nothing saved up for college. I held onto every single dollar you ever gave me. I'm an honest cop, okay? Use it to pay for books or something. Get some sleep, kid. I've been reassigned, but I'll be in touch. Take care of yourself and that pretty girlfriend of yours." Jake turned and left, but Michael wasn't so sure he would ever see his friend again. He counted the bills inside and was amazed that Jake had held onto that much money for him. He was a really good friend.

The following day held more surprise visitors. Laurie, Neal, and Chris came by together to see him. They filled him in on the random nothings of life in Riverside, but it was nice to just talk with them. They were a great group of people, now that he had taken the time to get to know them. He was going to miss their company now that the crisis was over.

"Anyway," Laurie said. "If you're still in here over the weekend we'll come back and visit."

"Oh, you don't have to," Michael said. "I know you guys would rather not be seen with me. I understand, but I really am glad you came today."

Neal paused by the door. "You don't get it, do you? We came because we're *your* friends now, for life. You showed us the old Michael, and you risked your life to save Jo. Face it, you're never getting rid of us now!"

"Nope!" the others chimed in. "Friends for life!"

"Aye," Chris added. "We're brothers now, and don' ye be fergettin' it!"

Michael's eyes misted a little and he faked a yawn to cover it, but they weren't fooled. Laurie came over and kissed his forehead.

"Get some sleep, you've earned it. We'll be back later."

17

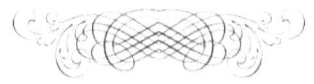

Julie came by to see him several more times before he was released from the hospital. The doctors wanted to make sure there was no subdural hematoma first or he would have had a stroke or died suddenly once he was home. She brought over some of his homework and helped him catch up. Even so, he knew he would have to go to winter school to completely catch up, there was no way he could take final exams next week. He had missed too much. But still, he appreciated Julie's efforts to help him.

"Mike," she started and he could tell this would be a serious discussion. "You said you believed you were irredeemable. Why is that?"

Michael debated lying to her, but he just couldn't. He wouldn't tell her everything, of course, but maybe just enough to appease her curiosity and move on to a different topic. "I'm a tough guy, a bully," he answered. "I know what I've done and how many people I've hurt. I'm not fool enough to think that saving a few girls from a fate worse than death is enough to erase all that red. But I'm gonna work real hard from now on to be different. I decided to be a social worker and help others get out of situations like mine. Maybe even rescue people from trafficking, I don't know... Maybe... maybe I can earn the chance to see you again."

He looked at her and tried to memorize every feature of her face. He would never tell her that he planned to leave Riverside just as soon as he completed enough credits to graduate. If he could catch up from his hospital stay that should be at the end of the semester. If not... well, he'd have to stay until the spring semester ended and graduate with the others.

"Michael," she started, but hesitated. He could see she was battling two opposing thoughts in her mind. She must have come to a decision because she took a deep breath and continued. "I know you feel that the things that have happened to you are your fault, but they're not! You are not responsible for anything that has happened to you. You must believe me. There is a hope and a future for you that you can't even imagine; it's so much *greater* than anything you could imagine. I could tell you about it, if you'd like." She tilted her head to the side and waited for his permission to continue.

Michael knew what she was hinting at, her faith, but he didn't want to hear about how God loved him and wanted to give him good things. He didn't believe he was worthy of all that and he knew that if Julie really knew everything he had done – how he caused his brother's death, how he betrayed his mother and forced her to leave, how he started his father down an alcoholic's path, how he had single-handedly destroyed his family... No, if she knew *that* she would agree with him that God could never love someone like him. He was too vile to love. She would figure it out someday, and then he would lose what little closeness they shared. No, her God wasn't for him. He was irredeemable, a nothing, and probably always would be. He could never do enough good deeds to earn God's favor, or win Julie's heart. He had always been a failure and likely would always be a failure. He poisoned everything he touched, and he didn't want to poison Julie, too.

"Don't bring me none of that Christian stuff, Julie," he

said. "It ain't for me. Besides, I got plans, I'll be alright."

"But Michael," she tried again.

"No!" He snapped at her, but instantly regretted it when he saw the crestfallen look on her face. "Listen, guys like me don't amount to much. Don't waste your time. If you want to leave, I understand and I won't come around again. But if you want to stay, then no more Christian talk."

Julie thought for a few minutes and then made her decision.

"I'll stay and help you finish your homework, but maybe it is best if we do spend some time apart. I'll always be here if you need me, Mike. Always. I care what happens to you and I will still try to help you find a way out of your situation. You have earned a place in our hearts; in mine especially. I'm not willing to let that go without a fight, but I will give you your space. For now."

She offered him so much more than he could hope for, she wanted to stay friends and she admitted to keeping a special place in her heart just for him. Perhaps it was already too late to spare her...

"Thank you," he responded. "I know that didn't come easy. Anyway, let's get back to work."

Michael was released from the hospital on December ninth, but no one was there to pick him up. He was forced to call one of his new friends and chose to call Neal. He hated that he had to share an intimate part of his life with another outsider, but his dad never came to visit him and refused to take him home from the hospital. In fact, no one had heard from his father in several days. Michael hoped his dad wouldn't be home for several more, he was still in a lot of pain and on crutches.

His sprained ankle had healed quickly, but the broken one was taking its time. Probably because he had to walk on it to escape. Everything else was either healed or almost healed. He *had* been in the hospital for four weeks. He didn't want another confrontation with his father until he was completely healed. He knew his father would be furious at all the attention Michael had garnered.

"Hey, buddy!" Neal walked into his hospital room with a big smile on his face. "Glad you're finally getting out of here, huh? We sure are! We're planning a Christmas party and you would be missed if you didn't come. How 'bout it? Next weekend at Laurie's place. I can pick you up!" He patted Michael gingerly on the shoulder and awaited a response.

"Uh, yeah, sure, I guess." Michael didn't know what to think. He never expected to be friends with that group at all, let alone be missed by them! What a huge change a few months made! Neal grabbed his few belongings and the nurse escorted them out to Neal's car. It was an uneventful ride home, but the conversation was pleasant.

When Neal pulled up at Michael's house and opened the door for him they were greeted by rank smells and a demolished living room.

"Whoa! What happened here?" Neal asked.

"I haven't been home to clean it. My dad works long hours. It's no big deal, won't take long to clean up." Michael just wanted Neal to leave, so he blew it off as a normal occurrence in his home. The truth was that he was even more afraid for his dad to come home. He needed to heal up quickly and straighten things up before his dad returned. Thankfully, Neal took the hint and left without too many more words.

Michael started by opening up a few windows to circulate the air, and then he got to work picking things up and putting them away. The task took hours, but eventually he was able to clear a path around the house and clean up the furniture. The rest would require two working legs, so it would have to wait. He was exhausted so he went up to his room without any dinner and fell asleep.

Michael's father did not return that day, nor the next.

In fact, Michael was beginning to worry about his father when three days had gone by with no word from him. Chris took him to physical therapy and to get his casts removed. The doctor said everything had healed well, but his ankle would always give him trouble.

Apparently it had started to heal incorrectly while he was unconscious and they had to reset it. Now it was just slightly out of place and would always ache. He hoped it wouldn't affect his ability to practice martial arts, he was really starting to excel at *bushidokan karate* and wanted to continue. The doctor said it was a possibility that he may have to give it up. Michael chose not to accept that and continued the exercises the physical therapist had shown him.

It was while he was doing those exercises one day that his father finally came home. And he was not happy.

"So there you are! Do you know what I've just been through?" Mr. Weber bellowed and his face turned red.

"Hey, Dad," Michael answered. "I was beginning to wonder where you went. The doctor says that I should-"

"I don't *care* what the doctor says! I was just arrested and 'held for questioning' by the police for domestic violence because of *you*! They think *I* did this to you! Now, where did they get *that* idea? Huh?" With each emphasis on his words he stepped closer to Michael and clenched his fists at his sides. Michael had seen his father angry before, but not like this. He was shaking uncontrollably and the saliva was pooling in the corners of his mouth making him look like a rabid animal. Michael was scared. Very scared. He took a step backwards to keep distance from his father.

"No, I don't know what you're talking about!" Michael tried desperately to explain. "What happened?"

Maybe if he could calm his father down a little they could get through this without violence.

"What happened? *What happened?*" His father was turning purple now. "Someone told them I *beat* you! When you show up at the hospital with broken bones and bruises they immediately arrest me! *Me!* That's *ridiculous*! *I never beat you!* What have you been *telling* people? You've ruined, completely *ruined* my good name! And after all I've done for you!"

Michael was angry now. Julie must have said something while trying to help him. She had to! Now he was going to get the beating of a lifetime when she should have just stayed out of it! His anger wasn't entirely with her though, he couldn't stay angry with her for long. She was trying to save him, he understood that, but she didn't know what she was doing and now look at what happened.

They arrested his father while he was in the hospital! Michael supposed that when it was discovered how he came by his injuries they released Mr. Weber, but did they stop and think about what it would mean for Michael? Apparently not, because here he was facing his father in a state that he had never seen before.

It was clear he had been drinking, maybe ever since he was released. There was no way to tell. Michael knew he needed to get out of there and fast. He backed away another step and turned to leave out of the back door, but his father stopped him by yanking on his bad arm. Michael felt the pulling against his still tender clavicle. *Please, don't break it again*, he prayed. To whom he had no idea, but if anyone was up there listening he would pray. *Please help me get out of here! Please! You came through once, will You help me again? I know I don't deserve it, but please!*

"Where do you think you're going, filth!? *I'm not finished with you yet!* You think you can go out fighting and drinking and doing drugs and then tell the cops I beat you to get away with it, huh? Well I got news for you; *NOT THIS TIME!*" His father took a swing, but Michael ducked.

"Hold on a minute!" Michael couldn't believe his father just accused him of fighting, doing drugs and

199

drinking! He was a problem child, yes, but he had his limits! The code of martial arts was strong, it was honorable. He never went against the code, never! Even when he told people he got into fights it was a lie, he never actually fought anyone. It was just a ruse to explain the things his own father did to him. He wouldn't stand there and let his father say such things to him. Not anymore. Today, he would stand up for himself, no matter the cost.

"I don't drink!" Michael yelled. "I don't get into fights; that was just to hide the truth of what *you* do to me! And I don't do drugs! I take *care* of myself. Something *you* should be doing! I'm your *son!*" He stepped closer to his father and wagged a finger under his nose.

"*You* should be providing for *me*, not the other way around," Michael continued. "You should *defend* me, not beat me! And yes, you *DO* beat me! It's abuse! And I'm not taking any more of it!"

He pulled his arm back to punch his father, something he swore he would never do. He was taught in karate class to respect his elders, never to raise a fist against a superior, to use his skills to defend the weak, and to use violence as a last resort only; but right now, he couldn't think of any of that. Right now, he was blinded by rage and years of pent up anger and hostility.

Right now, he just wanted to hurt his father like his father had hurt him. He gathered all his strength and launched.

18

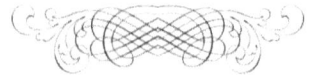

Julie could hear the yelling before she even got out of the car.

She didn't know what to do, though. Should she run in and try to break things up? Should she call the police? Should she call her parents? She sent up what she called a 'bullet prayer' to the Lord. *Lord, please show me what to do! Help him, please!* With her trust firmly planted in the Lord she got out of the car. As she approached the front door she dialed the police and begged them to hurry to Michael's home, that she could hear a terrible fight, and that Mr. Weber was known to beat his son. They promised to be there within five minutes. Julie didn't think Michael had that much time.

She raced up the walk and tried the door, it was unlocked and slightly ajar. No wonder she could hear so well. She entered the house just as Michael pulled back to strike. She knew he would regret the act so she grabbed his arm and stopped him from hitting his father.

"No, Mike," she implored. "Stop this, please! Just come with me, please, Mike! Please!"

"Who the heck are *you*?" Mr. Weber roared. "*Get out of here!*" He swung his fist to strike Julie. Michael ran in front of her at the last moment and threw her to the ground. He took the full force of the blow and fell backwards several feet. Julie gasped and hurried over to him. He was out cold. Completely knocked out by the blow. Before she could revive him, however, she was grabbed from behind and forcibly turned to face Mr. Weber.

"Answer me, wench! Who are you! What right do you have to come into my home? *My home!?*" He squeezed her arm to the point where it started to hurt. He grabbed her other arm and shook her. Hard. She was getting woozy from the constant back and forth motion. She could feel her brain rattling from the force of his exertions. She knew she had to break free, and fast!

Is this what Michael had to endure day after day? We

have to get out of here! But Mr. Weber wouldn't let go. She could smell the sickeningly sweet scent of liquor on his hot breath as he shouted at her. His mouth was foaming and the string of expletives coming from his moist lips was appalling and disgusted her clean through. And yet, still he shook her.

She took a chance that he was so drunk that he could easily be thrown off balance and so she kicked the side of his knee inward. It was enough for him to loosen his hold on her and she broke free. She ran to Michael and tried to drag him to the door, but he was too heavy for her. Mr. Weber lunged at her and knocked her to the ground. He pinned her shoulders and used his feet to hook her legs. She couldn't move. He bent over her and screamed in her face.

"You'll pay for that you little –" he shouted. "*I'll make you pay for that!*" He picked her head up and banged it on the floor, clumsily. Again. And again. Julie couldn't think straight, but she knew she had to stay conscious. Michael's life depended on it, not to mention hers. She had to break free!

She twisted from side to side, struggling to break his hold on her, but he was twice her size easily. He continued to attempt banging her head on the floor and she was quickly losing focus, but kept moving her head from side to side in order to keep him from getting a solid grip. *No! Michael needs me! I can't leave him here, I won't! Fight!* She took a deep breath and screamed!

Michael heard a bone-chilling scream and came awake with a start. His head was swimming, and he couldn't remember where he was at first. Then he remembered. His father was home. An urgency gnawed at him. Something was wrong... something... no, some*one*! *Julie!* He forced his mind to focus and saw his father on top of the love of his life. Michael's strength knew no bounds and all he saw was red. He launched himself at his father and rained down vengeance with the fury of an alpha wolf protecting his pack. He couldn't think of anything but saving Julie. He had to stop his father from hurting her. He was hurting her! Michael's worst fears came to life when he saw his father slamming her head on the floor. *He was hurting her!* What would have happened to her if he hadn't woken up? He didn't want to think of it, and he kept pummeling his father.

With each blow he released a little bit more of his anger and resentment, a little bit more of his pain. Eventually he noticed someone was trying to pull him off of his father. *Father? What does that even mean anymore...* he thought as he continued to lash out. But this person was extremely persistent and he finally decided to see who it was and what they wanted. It was Julie with tears streaming down her face.

"No, stop," she pleaded. "Please stop, you don't want to do this, I know you! Michael, please!"

He stopped and stared at her. "Julie?" He looked around and saw that his father was a bloody mess and completely unconscious. He felt for a pulse and found one. Now that his head had cleared and the rage was spent he was afraid he had killed him. "What happened...? He hurt you! Are you alright, my angel? Are you alright?" He reached for her and held her face in his hands. They were covered in blood, and he wasn't sure whose blood it was, but he didn't care. He needed to know she was alright.

"I'm alright, I'm alright. Just a headache, I'm not bleeding. I'm alright." She said it over and over again as if to convince herself, not Michael. He held her close and rocked her gently, kissing her cheek again and again. He could have lost her! Never! He would never let that happen! He'd lost too much already, Tom, Mom, Dad... His life, ultimately, was gone forever, but he wouldn't lose Julie. Not Julie. He would protect her, he would! He... he... he realized that he could never protect her. Not like he wanted. He couldn't even protect Tom...

He released his hold on her and crumbled into her lap as the tears streamed down his face. Julie rocked him gently and let him cry. He started muttering incoherently until the police arrived a couple of minutes later.

They questioned Michael and Julie while the paramedics revived Mr. Weber. Once they were certain he was out of danger they took him away in handcuffs, arrested for domestic violence. This time there were witnesses. Julie and a few of the neighbors could attest for what transpired. Michael didn't know what that meant for him and his father. All he knew was that Julie was safe. He was safe. At least for one more night.

The paramedics left after checking Julie and Michael for injuries, and the police offered to take him to a foster care home for the night, but he didn't want to go. He begged them to just let him stay in his own home for the night, but since he was still a minor they would not allow it. Julie offered to take him home with her and once they contacted her parents they released him into Dr. Hathaway's protection. Michael grabbed a few items including his guitar, and they left his house of horrors.

When they arrived at Julie's house Mrs. Hathaway rushed out and embraced Michael in the biggest hug he had ever received. He could see she had been crying, but it wasn't that that surprised him. It was what she said that rocked his world.

"Oh, my poor boy! I've been worried sick about you since the police called! Are you alright? How could someone *do* something like this to such a wonderful person? How could he *do* this!? Doesn't he see how precious you are? Come inside, son, I've got a room all prepared for you. You'll be safe here."

Julie's mother must have lost her mind, that was it. Surely she didn't know anything at all about what he had done in the past. If she did, she would never have said those things and been so comforting to him. Precious? No, he wasn't precious, he was worthless. She would learn someday and all this love and support would disappear. But for now he wanted to enjoy it. He would tell them tomorrow. He must have looked confused, though, because she spoke again.

"Michael, sweetheart," she said and looked lovingly at him, just like his own mother used to do before he sent her away. "I know you feel like you deserve the things that have happened to you. And some of the things you have done were really bad, but no one," she turned his face to hers, "look at me. *No one* deserves this! We figured it all out and what we couldn't piece together

Julie filled us in on. I spoke the truth, you *are* precious! Believe it because it's the truth! *We* love you! Now, come inside. I fixed some hot chocolate for you."

But Michael couldn't move. He broke down and wrapped his arms around Mrs. Hathaway. He could not stop the tears from falling, it was so nice to be loved! "You really believe that, don't you? Even though I caused so much pain for so many people? I'm irredeemable, I have accepted that. I know I am! I know it!"

Mrs. Hathaway held his face in her hands and shook her head. "My precious boy, you are not irredeemable! The Lord has already paid the price for you! All you have to do is accept it and believe Him when He says He loves you! And He does! So much more than anyone on this earth does, more than I do, more than my husband does, more than Jo does. And so much more than Julie does." With that she pulled him into the kitchen to bring him a steaming mug of hot chocolate.

Dr. Hathaway came downstairs and told Michael that the guest bedroom was ready for him whenever he was ready to go to sleep. Michael thanked him and tried to shake his hand as he had been taught long ago, but Dr. Hathaway just pulled him into a hug. A hug that spoke of his love for Michael and all that he had been through. As he released him Dr. Hathaway whispered in his ear,

"You're safe now, son. I won't let anyone hurt you ever again. You are my son, now and always. You risked your life again and again for my daughters. I will risk my life for you. That's a promise." With a final pat on Michael's back and a genuine smile, both he and Mrs. Hathaway went upstairs.

As he turned to sit down again, an incredulous look on his face, he noticed Julie beaming up at him.

"They really mean all that, don't they?" Michael asked her as he sat down and took a sip from his mug.

"Of course they do!" Julie exclaimed. "Don't you believe them?"

"No, I don't, JuJu," he shook his head. "They must not know how vile I am. I ruined everything, just like my father said. I killed Tom. I sent Mom away. I made Dad drink. I destroyed it all! Everything I touch withers and dies. You tell them, make them understand that I'm not worth it. I'm irredeemable, unlovable. I'm too messed up. Make them understand before it's too late!"

In response Julie rose from her seat and went upstairs. Michael was confused for a moment and thought he had sent her away, too, but she came back down with a book.

"I want you to read something, Mike," she said and opened the book. He could see now that it was a Bible.

She opened it to somewhere in the middle and pointed to the verses she had highlighted because she wanted him to read them. "Here, the highlighted verses. Read it out loud, please, and really think about what you're reading."

He took the book and glanced over the verses then started to read, "'Fear not, for I have redeemed you; I have called you by name, you are mine. When you pass through the waters, I will be with you; when you walk through fire you shall not be burned, and the flame shall not consume you...Because you are precious in my eyes, and honored, and I love you...' It's nice... Who said that, this Isaiah person?"

"No," she answered, "God said that and it's a message to each and every one of us. Don't you see, Michael? God truly does love you! Yes, even you! You are precious to Him and like my mom said, whatever penalty you think you deserve He has already paid it. All you have to do is accept it. Just tell Him you accept what He did for you and redemption is yours."

"Nah, can't be that easy. Julie," Michael shifted uncomfortably on the sofa. He wanted to believe this could be true, that he really *could* be redeemed, but it was just too fantastic to believe. "I've done some awful things! You just don't know!"

"Alright, then tell me. Confess the things that you have done and we'll talk about them, one by one if necessary. I promise to stay right here until *you* send me away." She took his hand in hers and covered it with her other hand. "I'm staying right here."

Michael battled with so many thoughts all at once. It was like there were multiple voices in his head all whispering different things; talk to her, trust her, don't say anything, stay away, she can't be trusted, she loves you, she won't abandon you, and so many others. But one voice sounded louder than the rest and it repeated a message that he had heard before, *"This is what I have for you, Michael, if you let Me."* He decided to trust that One because it was beginning to sound familiar and he longed to hear more of it. He briefly wondered if it was Jesus trying to reach him. *Jesus*, he thought, *is that You? Are you trying to reach me? Is this real?* He felt deep down inside that the answer was *"Yes!"*

"Julie, I killed my brother." He hung his head and wept, unashamedly.

"How do you think you killed him?" Julie asked. "I thought he died in a motorcycle accident. They told us that it wasn't his fault, he did everything right and was a cautious driver. Some drunk got behind the wheel and hit him at fifty miles an hour. They told us he died almost instantly. How are you responsible for that? Did you know the other driver?"

"No, I didn't," Michael answered. "But I killed Tom just the same. I told him to buy that bike! I helped him fix it up! I was the one that encouraged him to keep it instead of trading it in for a car! It's my fault he died!"

Julie reached over and pulled his head down to her shoulder. "No, Mike, it wasn't your fault at all. You did nothing wrong! Tom was a skilled driver, he knew what he was doing when he decided to keep it, and he knew what he was doing when he got on the road that night. It was the drunk driver's fault. The responsibility rests on his shoulders and his alone! I don't know why people drive drunk anyway. It causes so many people so much pain and suffering! Tom didn't do anything wrong and *neither did you*. The drunk driver did, Mike. *Believe* it!"

Jesus, he thought. *Are you still there? Is she right? Am I wrong to believe it was my fault?* Again he felt the answer resonate in his heart, "*Yes!*" For the first time in years, Michael felt that he could let go of the responsibility he had carried ever since Tom died. It really wasn't his fault! He knew it now!

"Then," he started again. "Am I responsible for my mom running away? She left because I found Tom's bike and started fixing it up. She hated me for that! She was so angry because that's what killed Tom and now here I was driving it. She hated me and ran away! I pushed her away and she left me… How could that *not* be my fault?"

"That wasn't your fault either, Mike," Julie said. "Your mom is a grown woman. She is responsible for the decisions she makes, good or bad. It was just bad timing that she left when she did, and she was very wrong for not explaining why she was leaving. She probably has no idea of the burden she placed on you by her actions! If we could find her then you can ask her these things yourself, but I guarantee that your mom still loves you and never meant for you to blame yourself. Did you guys go to counseling after Tom died?" At Michael's response in the negative she continued. "Then perhaps… maybe… your mom was extremely depressed and didn't know how to handle it… Maybe she left because she was trying to run from her pain, not from you. It's possible, right?"

"Yeah, I guess so," he said. "It never occurred to me that she left in order to get away from the pain. Tom left echoes, you know? Maybe she *couldn't* handle it…" He began to review the events leading up to his mother's disappearance, the hastily scribbled note saying she couldn't take it anymore, and the years that followed. The picture of his past was becoming clearer. He realized he was not responsible for Tom's death and now he knew he didn't force his mother to leave. That left just one last lingering doubt.

"What about my dad, though," he asked. "He is so angry with me for everything that has happened. He blames me for Tom dying and Mom leaving. He says so often enough... Why would he say those things if they weren't true? There must be *some* truth to it all... He says I'm worthless and that I caused all of his suffering. I mean, he's my dad, you know? He has to be right about some of it at least..."

"He's wrong about all of it, hon," Julie said and started to stroke his cheek. She kissed him gently on his forehead. She was also smoothing his hair and he had never felt anything so wonderful. It was just like when she showed concern over his bruised ribs a while back. He could just rest here for eternity and it would be heaven. She slowly rocked him back and forth.

"Oh Michael," she said and it was evident that she had started crying. She kissed his forehead again. "He was wrong about *all* of it! He never learned how to deal with his own pain, just like your mom. Don't you see? Each of you ran away, but in different forms. You turned to acting out and becoming a bully. Your mom literally ran away. Your dad turned to alcohol. You all ran away in a different manner. You all needed to talk to someone

215

about your pain and grief over losing Tom. You must have loved him very, very much. After nearly losing Jo, I think I can understand the depth of your pain. But listen to me, hon," There, she said it again. She called him 'hon' and he thought no word sounded as sweet. "None of that was your fault. You did *not* kill Tom. You did *not* send your mother away. You did *not* force your dad to drink. You did *not* ruin your family. You *did not deserve* to be beaten. You *did not deserve* any of this. Believe me, I speak the truth. Read these words over again and let them reach your heart."

He read them again and let the words sink in. "Fear not, for I have redeemed you; I have called you by name, you are mine. When you pass through the waters, I will be with you; when you walk through fire you shall not be burned, and the flame shall not consume you...Because you are precious in my eyes, and honored, and I love you..." He had certainly been through the fire, but he was still alive. He had seen his fair share of rough waters, but he never drowned. Could it be true? Could God really love someone like him? Before he even finished the thought he felt the answer in his heart, *"Yes! I love you! Come to Me, Michael, my precious child!"* The longing he felt deep in his soul to run to the voice in his soul was powerful and all consuming.

216

"Julie," he said. "I keep hearing this voice in my head. Saying, 'Come to me.' So… what do I do? It's your Jesus, right? I mean, like, God is speaking to me right? So, what do I do?"

"Yes, God is speaking to you. Did you know that He led a sinless life and yet He was sentenced and killed as a criminal? Just like you are not responsible for Tom's death, or what your parents did, but you paid a terrible price. He paid the ultimate price for our sins; yours and mine and everyone else that ever lived or ever will live. He died in our place. I read it once like this, 'He came to pay a debt that He did not owe, because we owed a debt that we could not pay.' It's true. We could never pay the penalty for our sins, but He could because He is God.

He loved – and loves – us so much that He was willing to die for us. He loves *you* so much that He was willing to die for *you*. And even after He died, He rose again and created a way for us to spend all eternity with Him in heaven. All you have to do is accept it and believe."

"Yeah, I heard that story when I was a kid. It's coming back to me now… The penalty for sin is death, no matter the sin, from a white lie to murder, it's all sin and all punishable by death. We could never pay the penalty for each sin that we commit. We only have one life and can only die once, which would leave other sins unpaid for…

Yeah, I remember now. So, what do I do to accept it? There's a special prayer, right?"

"Sort of. There are no special words, only a special feeling. A deep commitment to what you are praying. If you truly believe, I'll walk you through the prayer. Are you ready?" Julie could not contain the smile on her face. She was beaming from ear to ear, just like in the hospital. A smile to light up the cosmos for millennia. Michael loved seeing that smile, it was infectious. And deep in his soul he felt God smiling, too.

"I'm more than ready!"

"Then repeat after me," Julie said and started the prayer that would bring Michael home. "Dear Jesus, I know that I am a sinner. I have done terrible things. I know that there is a price to pay for all the things that I have done, but I also know that You have already paid that price. You took my place, even though You were sinless, because I owed a debt I could not pay. I can't begin to comprehend that much love, but I accept it. I accept the gift that You have given me by suffering on the cross, and dying in my place. I believe that You are the Son of God. I believe that you *are* the Lord God. I believe that You died and rose again. I believe that even now You are in heaven preparing a place just for me. Please come into my heart and save my soul from an eternity apart from You. Help me to be more like You. Thank you, Lord, for loving me that much! Amen!"

A burden was lifted from his shoulders as he prayed and for the first time in a long time, Michael smiled.

19

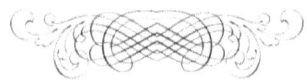

Michael stayed at the Hathaway house for several days, and learned from each of them about Jesus. Even Jo, who was overjoyed that her hero was safe, shared what she had learned about Jesus since she was kidnapped. She was still going to counseling and was doing much better. Her nightmares had lessened, but she was still afraid to talk to new people.

Michael, too, had started counseling sessions and was really doing well. He was learning how to process all that had happened, and how to channel his anger and anxiety in healthier ways. They had taught him how to use music to channel what he was feeling. He decided to use his ballad as a memorial to Tom, and rewrote the lyrics. It proved to be very therapeutic, and "Taken Too Soon" was cherished by the Hathaway's when he played it for them. When Sunday came around he was looking forward to going to church with the Hathaway's. As he came downstairs he noticed that everyone was helping prepare breakfast.

"Is there anything I can do to help?" Michael asked.

"There sure is! How are you at frying eggs?" Mrs. Hathaway asked.

"Fair to middlin' as my grandmother used to say." He found a frying pan and pulled out the eggs from the refrigerator. "Sunny side, scrambled, over medium?" The Hathaway clan just looked at each other and answered all at once.

"Scrambled!" Dr. Hathaway said.

"Over medium!" Jo said.

"Over easy for me!" From Julie.

"Oh, sunny side, please!" From Mrs. Hathaway.

"Scrambled with cheese!" This last from Josh who was home for Christmas.

"Oh, cheese! Yeah, that sounds good. Add cheese to mine, please!" Dr. Hathaway added.

Michael just laughed and said, "Okay, but it may take me a bit!" He loved that the family all pitched in to make Sunday breakfast. He loved that he could join them even more.

Finally everyone had the eggs they ordered and breakfast could begin. They clasped hands as Dr. Hathaway said a simple prayer. Michael had never had home fries before and was eager to see if Julie could cook. Could she! They were fantastic and he had several helpings before he realized he was eating too much.

"Sorry, they're really good…" he apologized.

"No problem," Julie said and laughed. "Glad you like them. My specialty. No one makes them as well as I do!"

"You'll be joining us for church, right?" Mrs. Hathaway asked.

"Um, yeah, I'd love to! Do I have to wear anything special?"

"Not at our church, just look nice. Well… *nicer.*" Julie winked, and he knew she was teasing. He had gotten a haircut and no longer wore the torn jeans or paint-stained shirts or combat boots. But he did still have his leather jacket. He wasn't parting with that!

A few minutes later Neal and Chris came by and it was time to go to church. With Josh home there wasn't enough room in the family minivan, so Julie opted to drive Neal, Chris, and Michael.

"Hey buddy," Neal said. "Got something for you." He handed Michael a small gift bag. When he opened it he was shocked to see a leather-bound Bible inside with his name embossed in silver at the bottom corner.

"Neal..." he started. "I... I... Thank you... This means more to me than I can put into words. My own Bible!"

"Yeah, yeah," Neal replied. "Don't go getting all girly on me!" They laughed and went out to Julie's car.

Wow! My own Bible! Michael thought. *My life has certainly changed. It's all thanks to You, Lord. Thank You for finding me!*

"Are you excited for the Christmas party?" Julie asked Michael as he was packing his few things into a duffle bag.

The trial for his father was finally over and he was convicted to several years in prison. Mrs. Mayweather volunteered to take guardianship of Michael, and after a thorough search for his mother it was approved. Apparently, they had found her but she didn't want to come back or resume responsibility for Michael.

It broke his heart, but he realized that maybe she was stuck in her grief just like his father was. He prayed for both of his parents daily and would continue to do so until they found their way back. He would be there for them, when they were ready.

"Yeah, I really am," he answered. Laurie had decided

to postpone her party until a few days before Christmas to give Michael a chance to process everything that had happened. He appreciated what she had done for him. It still amazed him that people could care this much for him. "I'm even more excited that you're my date!" He snuck a quick kiss.

Things with Julie were going well. Better than he expected, and far beyond what he had hoped for just a few short months ago. He enjoyed sitting beside her at church and being able to hold her hand. They did devotions together and he even volunteered for several upcoming church events with her.

He liked her church and couldn't believe how many of the teens in the youth group welcomed him in, even the ones he had terrorized! When he asked them why they were so willing to accept him they simply said that they had been praying for his salvation and were overjoyed that they could call him brother now. He had never experienced such open acceptance. How many people had been praying for him? Even Mrs. Mayweather admitted to praying for him often. He was surrounded in prayer all along. It still blew his mind!

He was even more excited to share Christmas with his new family. He had used some of the money Jake had returned to him to buy a present for each of them. He

224

hoped that they liked his gifts and wouldn't think him foolish. *No, Weber*, he thought to himself. *They ain't like that. They will love their gifts because they love you. That's all you've ever wanted anyway, to be loved.*

"Earth to Michael," Julie said. "Hey! You'd better hurry up! We'll be late!" She rushed out of his room to finish her own preparations.

Laurie had to change the guest list since some of her friends were out of town for the holiday. He felt bad about that until she admitted that the people she really wanted to be there would be; Julie, Neal, Chris, David, and him. She said she would have cancelled it altogether if he couldn't be there. She wanted him to have a nice Christmas, no matter what. He vowed to be there with bells on. And he meant it, too! He grabbed the sleigh bells from the dresser and hurried downstairs.

The walk to Laurie's was a pleasant one. It was cold and it had snowed overnight, but the sidewalks were clear and the stars were shining bright.

"I never thanked you," Michael said as he looped Julie's arm through his.

"What for?" She asked.

"For saving my life. In more ways than one. If it weren't for you... Well, I have no idea where I'd be. I had planned on graduating early and skipping town after

225

Christmas. I wasn't going to say a word to anyone, I was just going to disappear. Then you took a chance on a guy like me. Because of you my whole life has changed. I have a safe place to call home. My father has finally been brought to justice. My mother has been found. I have friends. I found my Savior. I have a future now. One that I hope includes you."

"Jeremiah, twenty-ninth chapter, eleventh verse. Do you know what it says?"

"Uh, sorry, no..." Michael admitted.

"That's okay. You're learning a lot all at once. It says, 'For I know the plans I have for you, declares the Lord. Plans to prosper you and not to harm you, plans to give you hope and a future.' He has a plan for each of us. He tries to give us His dreams for our lives, but we often choose a different path. Sometimes He gives us a glimpse of what He has for us. It's up to us to recognize it and seek His will. He knew from the moment you were born that all these things would happen. I'm sure He was overjoyed when you finally accepted the gift He was offering. I know I was!"

"Wait, back up," Michael said. "He sometimes lets us see what He has for us?"

"Yeah, to some people, why?"

"Oh no reason, just confirmation on something. Don't

worry about it." He was astonished. Those images he had seen again and again, the voice saying, *"This is what I have for you, Michael, if you let Me."* All of it, it was his Lord and Savior giving him a picture of the plans He had for Michael and Julie! He finally understood now!

The newborn baby, the office where he helped people in need, Julie wearing his ring; it was all a possible future for him if he would only let God work in his life! He could spend his life with Julie! It was all the assurance he needed. He would let God work in his life. He wanted that future with Julie. He wanted to help others in need just as she helped him. He would turn things around and use his experiences to bring comfort and the gospel message to others in pain and suffering. He repeated the verse Julie mentioned over again in order to commit it to memory. God had been moving in his life all along, Michael just didn't know it!

Julie was amazed at the changes in her life in recent months. Here she was walking beside Bruce Weber! But he wasn't Bruce Weber anymore. The person he was for the past three or four years was gone forever. In his place was a young man who loved the Lord and wanted to turn his life around. He was Michael Weber now, and he loved her. At least, she was pretty sure he did. He still had yet to *say* it to her... Now that she thought about it, did she even love him back?

She looked up at him as they approached Laurie's house. She paid careful attention to the strong curve of his chin, the way his hair – now a little shorter and not dyed black or spiked – kept falling over his brow no matter how many times he pushed it back; the soft slow smile that spread across his face as he caught her staring. *Yeah*, she thought to herself, *I love him. If he ever says it to me I would say it back.* She wondered what he meant by "confirmation on something," but didn't have time to dwell on it. They had arrived at Laurie's house and it was time to celebrate the birth of her Savior!

Laurie greeted them at the door and handed both of them a cup of homemade eggnog, minus the alcohol of course.

"Come in! Come in! Everyone else is here!" She ushered them in and took their coats. There was music and laughter and lots of food! Julie had been to Laurie's Christmas party every year and still she was amazed at how much food Laurie and her mom prepared.

"Laurie!" she said. "How are we going to eat all of this?" But as she glanced back at the table the boys had already devoured half of it.

"What," Neal said around a mouthful of food. "Laurie

228

said we couldn't eat until you got here. You're here, so…" He turned back to the wonderful assortment of delectable dishes in front of him. Julie just laughed. It was the same thing every year.

After they had eaten their fill and exchanged gifts, Laurie said it was time to read the story.

"Story?" Michael asked.

"The story of Christmas. Why we as Christians celebrate this day. It's the story of how God became man and entered our world to save us." Laurie explained as she took the family Bible off the shelf. "David, why don't you start and we'll go around the room and each read a section. Michael, that means we end it with you!"

Julie watched Michael's face as the story was read from Luke chapter two. He was enraptured by how the little baby Jesus came into the world. When it was his turn to read he spoke with such awe that they all heard the story as if for the first time. Each of them was moved by the reverence with which he spoke, and remembered what it was like when they felt the same astonishment at the story.

"'When they had seen him, they spread the word concerning what had been told them about this child, and all who heard it were amazed at what the shepherds said to them. But Mary treasured up all these things and pondered them in her heart.'"

As he continued reading the last few verses of the story, Julie thought about verse nineteen. "Mary treasured up all these things and pondered them in her heart..." *What must it have been like for her, looking down at her newborn baby and seeing the trust in His eyes for His very survival? How much more awestruck must she have been to realize she was staring at the face of God! I never thought about it before, but it must have been quite a humbling experience!* She began to wonder what she would think and feel when she became a mother for the first time.

Suddenly she got a vision of a little baby in her arms. She looked up to see Michael standing near looking down at her and their newborn. She was sure the little baby in her arms was theirs. The ring on her finger proved it.

Julie blinked and had a strong sensation that she had just been given a beautiful gift. One she felt completely unworthy of. But deep in her soul she knew that if she followed the Lord's will, that vision would be her future. She looked up to see Michael looking at her with such love and adoration that her cheeks flamed and she looked away. Had she spoken out loud? It was like he knew what she had been thinking!

He reached over and took her hand in his big strong one. She leaned against him while they sang the old Christmas carols she loved so much. On the walk home Michael and Julie dillydallied for a while, enjoying the crisp but pleasant evening.

"JuJu," Michael said and turned her to face him. "I have another present for you, a special one."

"What is it? Can it wait until Christmas, it's only two days away?"

"No, this one can't wait. I'm hoping this gift will set the tone for all our Christmases to come."

Michael bent down on one knee and pulled a little box from his pocket.

"This isn't an engagement ring, we're still too young for that, but it is a Promise ring. Julianne Marie Hathaway, I love you. And I promise to always love you. This ring is a symbol of my commitment to you and to our future. When the time comes and I ask you officially for your hand, will you say yes? I love you, JuJu and I want to spend the rest of my life walking beside you, hand in hand."

"Oh Mike!" Julie knelt down, too, and clasped his hands. She couldn't help but smile; her heart was full and overflowing. "I love you, too! Yes! When next you ask me, my answer is yes!"

A Note From The Author:

This book deals with some pretty intense issues! I chose to use teenagers as my characters in order to *reach* teens. While it is a work of fiction, it is also real life for so many people. Growing up is a scary business today and the more resources our youth have the safer they will be. These are issues that so many young people deal with on a daily basis and no one notices.

Human trafficking, either for sex or for labor, happens right under our noses in ways we never imagined, gangs in the inner city are a prime example. Johannah was just trying to make new friends, she never guessed that she was being pulled into an elaborate web of deception. How often do we find ourselves willing to yield on one or two seemingly small issues in order to be accepted by a group? If we're being honest with ourselves, too often.

Parents, know who your children are spending time with! Invite them over, offer to drive, let *your* house be the hangout spot. Make it fun and a place they all enjoy visiting. Provide that safe haven they are looking for and encourage each person that walks through your door as the Hathaway's do. Let your kids and their friends know that no matter what time it is, if they call you will answer and you will be there for them. For many of them, you may be the only one. My parents did this for me and I can tell you, it works! It works because it shows them how much you care.

Domestic violence and child abuse are also happening all around us every day. The Weber family went through a terrible tragedy and never sought help to process. They let their grief consume them and it destroyed their lives. This really *does* happen! When you know that someone is going through a difficult time listen to them, support them, guide them to healthy ways of coping. Be watchful of *any* unusual behavior and seek help! It may be the most difficult decision you ever make, but it could also save a life.

The last thing I want to leave you with is this: *do not try to solve the problem yourself!* What Michael did was wrong, he should have let the police handle matters and he suffered greatly for his mistake. If you suspect child abuse or trafficking your *primary* responsibility is to report it as soon as possible and then let the authorities handle it. If you don't know who to contact, then call 911 (in the USA). They will know what to do, but not unless you call. Please stay safe and be vigilant. Never go anywhere alone if at all possible. Protect yourself and your friends by staying informed and reporting cases of suspected abuse or trafficking.

Thank you for reading this book! I left some goodies in the following pages, enjoy!

JULIE'S FAMOUS HOME FRIES

4 – 6 Large Potatoes, washed and peeled

1 Red or Yellow Onion, sliced

1 Tbsp. Paprika (additional paprika to taste)

Salt, to taste

Pepper, to taste

1/4 Cup Oil

Slice potatoes 1/8 to 1/4 inches thick. Heat oil in a large non-stick frying pan until warm. Evenly place potatoes and onions in pan. Fry on medium-high heat five minutes. Gently turn potatoes and sprinkle with salt, pepper, and paprika. Turn potatoes to coat. Continue frying on medium-low heat, covered, stirring frequently until potatoes are soft and onions are translucent, about twenty minutes. Add additional oil as needed to keep potatoes from sticking and drain excess before serving. Serves 4-6.

MICHAEL'S SPICY SLOPPY JOES

1 lb. Ground pork

1/2 Cup chopped green, red, and yellow bell peppers

1/2 Cup chopped red onion

1 Tbsp. brown sugar

1 Tsp. ground mustard

1/4 Tsp. salt

1/4 Tsp. pepper

1/8 Tsp. cayenne pepper

1/2 Cup ketchup

1 Tbsp. vinegar

1 Tbsp. Worcestershire sauce

1 (8-oz.) can tomato sauce

1 (14-oz) can diced tomatoes w/ chilies (drained)

6-8 large hamburger buns

In a large skillet combine pork, bell peppers, and onion. Heat on medium-high 8-10 minutes or until meat is cooked through. Drain. Add brown sugar, ground mustard, salt, pepper, cayenne pepper, ketchup, vinegar, Worcestershire sauce, diced tomatoes, and tomato sauce. Reduce heat to medium-low, cover. Continue simmering, stirring occasionally 15-25 minutes until flavors are well blended. Warm hamburger buns in microwave 10-15 seconds. Spoon generous portion of Sloppy Joe mixture on each bun. Serves 6-8.

"Taken Too Soon" (Michael's tribute to Tom)
Lyrics by Rebecca M. Norris

You were my first and
best friend
Swore we'd stick
together until the end
Having fun out in the
backyard
Growing up didn't seem
so hard

But you were taken too
soon

℞   Sorry I wasn't
there for you
Sorry I couldn't care for
you
Didn't get to say goodbye
Never thought that you
would die

And you were taken too
soon

I remember like it was
yesterday
When they told me you
had gone away
Mom and Dad couldn't
even move
I didn't know what I
should do

'Cause you were taken
too soon

℞   Sorry I wasn't
there for you
Sorry I couldn't care for
you
Didn't get to say goodbye
Never thought that you
would die

And you were taken too
soon

Life is different now that
you're gone
I find it difficult
sometimes to move on
But I remember how
things used to be
And I know someday I
will set you free

You were taken too soon

℞   Sorry I wasn't
there for you
Sorry I couldn't care for
you
Didn't get to say goodbye
Never thought that you
would die

You were taken too soon
You were taken too soon

DISCUSSION QUESTIONS

1. Michael Bruce Weber was a bully, but he wasn't always one. The circumstances in his life changed him and he reached out in a very unhealthy way. Have you ever had to face a bully? What did you do? Was that a healthy response or an unhealthy one?

_____

_____

_____

_____

_____

_____

_____

_____

_____

_____

_____

_____

_____

_____

2. Jo wanted so badly to be accepted by the older kids that she did whatever they asked her to do. Have you ever craved acceptance to the point where you compromised your principles? What was the result?

_____

_____

_____

_____

_____

_____

_____

_____

_____

_____

_____

_____

_____

_____

_____

_____

_____

3. Julie had a habit of taking on the world's problems. She always thought she could fix things herself, but she finally realized that some things were bigger than her. Have you ever faced a problem that was too big for you alone to handle? What did you do? Have you ever thanked those that helped you solve your problem?

_____

_____

_____

_____

_____

_____

_____

_____

_____

_____

_____

_____

_____

_____

_____

4. As parents, Dr. and Mrs. Hathaway felt it necessary to use tough love with their youngest daughter. Have you ever had to make a decision that was as painful to you as sending Jo away was for them? What process did you use to come to that decision?

_____

_____

_____

_____

_____

_____

_____

_____

_____

_____

_____

_____

_____

_____

_____

_____

5. Find a list of websites for domestic violence or human trafficking. Choose one to study and use the spaces on the following pages to record what stood out to you the most about this organization. (Their beliefs, mission statement, history, plan of action, resources, statistics, etc.) Was this information helpful to you? If you are ever faced with a similar situation will you know what to do and where to go for help?

_____

_____

_____

_____

_____

_____

_____

_____

_____

_____

_____

_____

_____

BEYOND THE PAGE

Find a local organization in your community that aids victims of abuse or trafficking and volunteer. Get to know the people you meet and hear their stories. Be a friend to them, you may just be surprised at the results! Bring a group of your friends, too, and you can all connect and grow together!

Be careful to protect the identities of the people you meet, too. Help keep them safe!

Find A Local Organization

Volunteer!

Find a community center or organization that aids victims of abuse or trafficking.

Start A Conversation

Talk!

Get to know the people you meet and hear their stories.

Be A Friend

Grow!

Learn as much as you can and be a listening ear for those you meet.

About the Author:

 Rebecca M. Norris is a lover of all things science fiction and fantasy. She even had a Lord of the Rings themed wedding! She currently resides in Kansas City with her husband, who is a fellow author, and their three children; happily enjoying the chaos that comes from being a mom. Mostly, Rebecca M. Norris is just your average woman who loves life and the people she shares it with, including you, her readers!

Visit her at rebeccanorrisstories.medium.com!

By Rebecca M. Norris

*The Legendary Adventures of Captain Grant Mason
Book One: Captain Grant Mason vs The Black Talons*

Grant Mason and his crew must fight their way through the Black Market Conglomerate to locate the Black Talons, the weapons dealers and mercenaries of the galaxy. Their assignment: acquire magnatomic particle dispersers from the Talons for use in the war against K'Lon. Simple right? Nothing is ever simple for Grant Mason...

Join Grant and his unique crew as they embark on an epic mission filled with intense danger, certain death, laughable mishaps, stunning surprises, and of course... legendary adventure!

The Legendary Adventures of Captain Grant Mason
Book Two: Captain Grant Mason vs The Supernova

Grant Mason thought he had the perfect crew. That is, until too many unfortunate mishaps involving his dinner changed his mind. Enter H'Eyli Galad, a half Nipoli half B'Rai with the disconcerting ability to blow things up when she's angered. And she was angry with Captain Mason! Nothing is ever simple for Grant Mason...

H'Eyli absolutely positively did not want to work for Grant Mason. He couldn't even pronounce her name correctly! And he had the audacity to tell her she was assistant chef, not head chef... The nerve!

Join Mason, H'Eyli and the crew of the O.N.S. T'Naan on an epic new adventure to rescue an abducted doctor amidst a group of mercenaries with a dark secret!

Book Three
Coming Soon!

One Final Breath

Even though his girlfriend is doing her best to convince him that Jesus is God, Brooks just wants to live his life, not tie himself to a church pew. Indigo is grateful her best friend doesn't browbeat her to follow Christ because the more she learns about science, the less she believes in God. Ilaria's husband has been concerned about her for some time. She and their oldest daughter belong to what he feels is a horrible cult. Somehow he has to find a way to reach both of them, before it is too late.

A short time later as their lives suddenly collide, Brooks, Indigo, and Ilaria discover they have already made the most important decision of their eternity. Unfortunately, it is the wrong choice. Now the battle for their souls is over. They have taken their final breath, their decision is irreversible, and there are no second chances.

One Final Breath shares the inspirational tale of three lost souls as their choices lead them down an unexpected path to the truth.

Finding Peter

Hannah – A young woman on a mission to find her best friend's murderer.

J.D. – A wealthy philanthropist who isn't what he appears to be.

Kaci – A crack-shot reporter determined to find the story of a lifetime.

Bryce – A college student in training to join the government as a white knight hacker.

Hannah Gracen needed some help and fast! Her best friend was killed, but the man accused - and sentenced to execution at midnight - is innocent. The only one that saw what really happened that night is a little boy named Peter.

But Peter has a secret. A secret he must keep in order to save the world, a world gone horribly awry. And someone is watching him, bent on his destruction. Can Hannah convince him to tell the truth no matter the cost? Will Peter's story set an innocent man free or condemn them all?

Peter must decide, and time was running out. Or was it...? Nothing is as it seems.

Four strangers embark on a journey that forever changes their lives. They will be tested in ways they never thought possible. Will they survive or perish? Who is the Man in Black? Who is Peter? What is the secret that drives the Emperor into a murderous state in order silence them? And more importantly, why do they remember events that haven't happened?

Finding Peter is an epic science fiction dystopian adventure novel by Rebecca M. Norris that will leave you hungry for more!

By Editor Scott Norris

Visit Scott at: scottnorriswrites.medium.com

The Chronicles of Solatia
Book One: Marno's Shield

In the country of Syren, young boys are becoming men in the time-honored tradition of the Age of Ascension Ceremony. Upon the conclusion of the ceremony, the King of Syren and the King of Maif sign a lasting treaty of peace. Marno, who just passed his Ascension, believes his future is bright.

Then a betrayal of epic proportions throws his world into chaos. Marno and his best friend, Tigrand, must sacrifice everything in a war they are ill prepared for... or lose it all forever.

Hardcover ISBN 979-8-9850976-1-0
Paperback ISBN 979-8-9850976-0-3
eBook ISBN 979-8-9850976-2-7

Book Two Coming Soon!

Check out our line of journals:

Books & Journals

a division of Duskraven Entertainment, LLC

Over 200 journals to choose from!

Order yours today!